ABRAM

THE CO

BY HENRY
BLACK

ABRAMACABRE: THE COLLECTION

Copyright © 2018 by Henry Black

First publishing 2018

ACKNOWLEDGEMENTS

A special thanks to one of my author friends for giving me the confidence to begin my writing, an anonymous friend for her ongoing support of my writing, and James for aiding me with the design and maintenance of the website.

CONTENTS

AN INTRODUCTION

Abramacabre began as a small project for me to further my writing skills and to create something that I enjoyed. I never expected for one moment that it would rise to the level of popularity that it has done. I am ever grateful to all of those people who have supported me and enjoyed my stories.

I have decided to publish my most well received stories as a collection for fans to own as their own. The collection includes my most well received stories that have garnered your support and attention, as well as four brand new stories that have not been published to Abramacabre yet. I really hope you enjoy.

For those people who have never heard of Abramacabre or Henry Black, I say hello and welcome to my world. Abramacabre is an online site where I publish two short horror stories every week. My aim is to create a subversion of the norm and to really explore the darkest corners of humanity and the human mind. I hope you enjoy these tails and are left horrified yet wanting more.

Henry Black

THE GIRL IN
THE BUNKER

Earth. The year 2105. The world has been ravaged by Nuclear War. Only few have survived. A bunker located just outside Greater London. The bunker was built underground when the war was announced. Luckily, the residents are among the lucky few alive. They were a married couple, Joshua and Alex. They built the bunker years before the war as they could see it coming. The whole country could. Tensions had been high since the twenty first century. Joshua and Alex had not been above ground in six years. The country was unsafe to travel to. Joshua had been gathering tanks of oxygen upon first getting the idea of building a bunker. Over the years, they had enough to last them a long time. Alex built an artificial greenhouse underground that provided UV lights and created more than enough crops.

It was a hot night. Joshua woke up in a pool of sweat. He climbed out of bed and made his way over to the sink to wash his face clean. The water trickled out in a pitiful stream. It hadn't rained for a while. The tank was near enough empty. Joshua had built a mass water tank and filtering system to make it safe to drink. After washing his face, Joshua could still not sleep. In the bunker, Alex had built a small glass dome on the surface and a ledge so that you could sit and gaze upon the sky and the world around you. Joshua perched himself on the ledge. The sky was extremely clouded over. Neither he or Alex had seen stars since the start of the war. A rattle from down in the bunker caused Joshua to jump.

'Alex? Is that you' Joshua whispered cautiously. A soft hum rang through the bunker. The hum of a person. Joshua made his way into the bunker to find Alex sleeping soundly in bed. He examined the room but found nothing. Lying back into bed, Joshua decided to go to sleep.

The next night, the hum returned to the bunker. This time, Alex noticed the hum too. Joshua and Alex rose from their bed extremely startled. The hum appeared to be the humming of a small child. A small child humming her favourite lullaby. Alex turned on the torch and examined the room.

'Joshua do you hear that?'

'Yeah I do, I heard it last night when I couldn't sleep. What the hell is it?'

'I have no idea. Stay here. I'm going to go and investigate.' Alex rose from the bed and dressed himself in a robe. The torch panned around the main room of the bunker but there was nothing that could explain the humming. Something scuttled across the bunker directly in front of the torch light.

'What was that!' Joshua exclaimed. Panic dominated his voice. He sat up in the bed and clutched the covers against his face. 'It went into the greenhouse.' Alex's heart was ready to burst from his chest and run away. He made his way to the door. His hands trembled, and his knees were about to give in. Joshua rose from the bed and dressed in his robe before fearfully joining Alex at the door. They reached for the handle together and pushed it open.

The automatic lights blinked into existence and illuminated the rows and rows of plants and crops. The room was a lot larger than the living room to make space for the food they needed to survive. Alex made his way down the first aisle of crops with Joshua following him sheepishly. Alex called out but there was no response. A faint sound of clattering and scattering feet echoed across the room. Alex chased after them, leaving Joshua behind. Joshua tried to chase Alex but became lost in a maze of crops and trees. The heat of the greenhouse made him sweat through his robe and tire easily. He paused for breath at the end of an aisle of crops. The humming had now stopped which relieved Joshua's nerves. Now, a faint, ghostly echo rang across the room. A child's singing.

'Now I lay the down to sleep. I pray the Lord my soul to keep. For if I die before I wake, that's one less test I'll have to take.' Repeated itself on a loop. Each time becoming increasingly twisted and eerie. Joshua crouched to his knees and placed his head in his hands. Desperate for anything other than the haunting melody to occupy his mind. He banged at his head. 'Make it go away' he pleased. The bunker was impenetrable. How had someone got in?

'Joshua? Joshua! Where are you?' Alex distantly shouted. He was too far away to help his husband. Joshua rose from his slump as the singing got louder. Louder. Closer. Something was there. Coming towards him. Joshua swivelled around, desperate to locate the source of his nightmarish plagues, his heart beating ever faster. There she was. Half the way down from the aisle of plans opposite Joshua. A girl. She could be no older than 8. Her hair muddied and greasy. Her skin cut and bruised. Joshua approached her, despite his fears.

'H-h-hi th-there sweetie. A-Are you okay? How d-did you get in here? Are your f-family nearby? Do you need help?' He reached out a trembling, but supportive hand. She continued singing as she pierced his soul with her macabre stare. Nothing lay behind her eyes. A blank stare to haunt Joshua's mind forever.

'Now I lay the down to sleep'

'I pray the Lord my soul to keep'

'For if I die before I wake,'

'That's one less test I'll have to take'

Over. Over. The song repeated itself. Joshua approached ever closer. The girl was stick thin. Her bones were visible on her arms and all over her body. Her face was ghostly. She was a phantom. Her eyes were locked on Joshua. The distant cries of Alex seemed to get further and further away. Joshua was now up close with the girl as she continued to sing the same verse over and over again. As he cautiously approached, the girl spirit launched herself at Joshua and wrapped her hands around his neck. She seemed to be draining the life from his body.

'Joshua! JOSHUA! Where are you!' Alex cried

'Now I lay the down to sleep'

'Joshua! I'm coming!'

'I pray the Lord my soul to keep'

'Joshua answer me!'

'For if I die before I wake,'

'I'm coming for you! You're going to be okay!'

'That's one less test I'll have to take'

Joshua's screams fuelled Alex to run faster. He needed to save his husband. Nothing in the world could stop him from protecting the one he loved. Not war. Certainly not an intruder. He ran through the greenhouse until he reached the aisle where the screams came from. Joshua gasped for air as every last breath was sucked from him by the girl's strong embrace. He began to feel faint. This was life or death. Alex needed to act immediately. He sprinted down the aisle and lunged at the girl to free his husband. Alex dived with the force of a Cheetah catching its prey.

He crashed hard on the floor. Filled with pain, he turned to see the girl was no longer clasping at Joshua's neck. He scanned the aisle of plants and she was nowhere to be found. Alex turned suddenly to see her standing directly behind him. He screamed as she slapped him across the face and howled a blood-curdling howl that left Alex in utter despair. Alex rose to his feet and ran to Joshua. He was struggling to breathe but he was still alive and okay. The two turned to discover that the girl had vanished yet again.

'Where the hell has she disappeared to?' Alex questioned angrily.

'I don't know but she's far stronger than she looks. She's inhuman' Joshua replied, still shook up and breathless from the incident.

'Whatever she is, we can't let her do this to us. This is our bunker. We work so hard to achieve what we have here. I will not stand by and let someone scare us out. We need to think of a plan to get rid of her. Alex and Joshua began to head towards the main quarters of the bunker. They held each other's hands so tight. Both were more terrified than they would have liked to admit. They approached the main door and stopped in sheer horror. Scratched into the metal walls, was a message for the two of them. How the girl had torn her way into the hard metal walls was beyond them both. They were too horrified by the message. It read:

'YOU CAN'T GET RID OF ME. THIS BELONGS TO ME NOW. IF YOU TRY AND STOP ME. YOU WILL DIE.'

Alex was now enraged. 'How dare she think she can threaten us like that. This is our bunker. She cannot control us. We need to think of a plan.' He wiped the sweat from his brow. 'We need to trap her so she can't slip away and then throw her outside.'

'Let's think of a plan in the morning. We're both too fatigued to successfully pull it off tonight. I'll lock the door to the greenhouse so she can't bother us in the main quarters tonight.' Joshua said through yawning. Alex agreed that this would be for the best and entered through into the main quarters. Alex checked around the quarters to make sure she was not there. Joshua locked the door and gazed through the porthole into the pitch black greenhouse. He became startled by a light suddenly flickering on and off. There she was again. The girl. Standing directly below the flickering light.

'Alex! She's back again. Come and see this.' Joshua shouted. Alex joined him at the porthole to see the girl standing there, perfectly still. She glared with her dead eyes right into Alex and Joshua's souls. The light flickered off. The light next to it in the direction of the door flickered on. There she was. Closer now. Alex and Joshua were comforted by the fact that she could not get through a locked door. The light flickered off. The next flickered on. There she was. Off. On. Closer. Off. On. Closer still. She now stood directly on the other side of the door to Alex and Joshua.

'Hah! Where are you going to go now? Can't get through a locked door can you!' Alex mocked her. He manually switched the greenhouse lights off, plunging her into darkness. Joshua and Alex both headed over to the bathroom area. Joshua decided to take a shower before getting back into bed because he was extremely clammy with sweat. Alex washed his face in the sink and readied himself for bed.

'Do you feel reassured now Josh?' Alex inquired. 'She can't get through the door. We can sort her out in the morning. All we have to do is quickly grab her before she slips away and throw her out of the hatch.'

'I do feel slightly bad for her. She is only a young girl. We don't know if it's safe above ground yet. Not fully. I do agree that she cannot stay here. You simply can't invade and then demand to be the sole owner of a sanctuary.'

'I know she's only young but she managed to get here. For all we know the rest of her family are waiting for the call that she has been given a home and they all pile in on us. Then what do we do? Our oxygen can't sustain more than two people. Our crops barely get us through.'

BANG. BANG. BANG. A loud rattle rang from the door to the greenhouse. Alex glanced over to see the girl still standing there on the other side of the glass. He ignored her and continued to prepare himself for bed. Joshua continued to shower and ignored her presence all together. The banging continued. Alex approached the door and banged back to signal to the girl to shut up. Alex tried to comfort himself with the reassurance that she could not break through a locked door. However, she was not as they had first assumed. To Alex's horror, she simply stepped through the door and into the main chamber. She picked up a piece of piping and slammed Alex in the head with it. He toppled to the floor, blood trickled down his face.

The girl approached Joshua in the shower who did not see her at first. He was horrified to turn around and see her watching him from the other side of the glass. He tried to exit the shower but she held the door closed.

'Alex! Help me! She's trapped me in. I can't get out. What do you want from us?' Joshua screamed. His face was flushed with panic. She grinned at Joshua menacingly. The shower filled with steam. Joshua cried in intense pain. She was turning up the temperature. Joshua did not know how but she was scolding him. He was burning in agony with no chance of escape. She locked eyes with him as she watched him suffer at her hands.

Joshua screamed in agony as the piping hot water burned his skin. He pushed on the door but it was to no avail. The girl was too strong. It didn't even budge. Alex lay on the floor extremely disorientated. His vision tainted with bloody and double images. All he could hear was the muffled scream of Joshua and knew he had to do something. He stumbled to his feet only to topple over due to dizziness. He was to weak and disorientated to do anything.

'Please leave him alone! Don't do this. We concede. The bunker is yours!' Alex slurred in desperation. He couldn't bear to hear the screams of his husband any more. He could not stand the pain. The girl turned form Joshua and looked directly at Alex. The water in the shower began to trickle to a halt. Joshua's screaming settled down. Alex could still not see him clearly to know if he was safe. His stomach twisted in knots. 'Let him go. Please. Please let him be free' Alex screamed in his head. He was too weak to say the words out loud. The girl stared directly at Alex and removed her grasp on the shower door, allowing Joshua to break free. Joshua was tomato red with steam rising from his smouldering body. He returned himself to the shower and blasted himself with cool water to avoid blistering. He shrieked at the top of his lungs with the displeasure that the burning caused him. The Girl dropped through the floor and disappeared right in front of them.

'Where did she go? Joshua are you okay? I can't see. I need help!' Alex cried. Joshua finished showering himself and immediately ran to the aid of Alex. He kneeled down and lifted Alex's head. He propped it up on a pillow before he

11

cleaned the wound and dashed around to find medical supplies to bandage the wound. Alex moaned pitifully as Joshua dressed the wound and helped him to his feet. Joshua lead him to the bed and tucked him in before washing the blood from his face.

'There you go. Try not to go to sleep for a while. Just get yourself comfortable and relax.' Joshua said as he stroked Alex's cheek ever so gently. 'I'm going to rub some cooling cream on my back, I won't be long.' He rose from the bed and over to the bathroom area to apply the cream.

'What are we going to do about the girl?' Alex croaked painfully. 'I said I'd surrender the bunker to her. Does that mean we have to leave now?' Joshua had never heard Alex sound so afraid before. In years of marriage, Alex had always been the brave one. The one who protected Joshua. Now the shoe was on the other foot and Joshua had to pretend he was not petrified beyond belief.

An hour or so passed and Joshua now laid in bed next to Alex, comforting him gently by rubbing his chest with the tips of his fingers. The room was bathed in a void of silence. It was almost too quiet. Joshua gazed around the room until he met with her eyes. This time she stood at the foot of the bed. Staring at the two of them. Alex saw her too. They both tensed themselves and sat up to distance themselves from her and to make a quick escape.

'Why are you doing this to us?' Alex moaned. 'What have we done to you?'

'I am suffering eternally because of you.' She declared in a clear, gentle tone.

'What do you mean? How?' Alex questioned.

'A year ago tonight. I came to your bunker seeking refuge. My family had been killed and I was about to meet their fate. I was hungry and cold. I hadn't eaten for days. I simply asked for a small amount of food but your husband turned me down.'

'What? Joshua is this true?' Alex turned to Joshua accusatively.

'I'm so sorry! We were having a shortage ourselves and were worried we weren't going to survive much longer. I couldn't risk it. I'm so sorry.' Joshua confessed, a guilty pang was present in his voice.

'Why didn't you tell me? We could have handled it together.' Alex was clearly hurt by Joshua's actions.

'I went away disheartened and collapsed not far away from your home. I died in pain because of your selfishness. Now I am doomed to wander your property for eternity and I will seek my revenge. I cannot bare to live an eternity knowing I am dead and the two of you continue to thrive.' The girl was now angered at Joshua and Alex.

'I am so sorry for what we did to you. If we had known the severity of your case we would have never turned our backs on you. Please forgive us.' Alex pleaded. He was heartbroken that a girl had died because of Joshua and he had no clue. The girl's face turned cold. She slithered up the bed until she was right in Alex's face.

'YOU WILL SUFFER FOR WHAT YOU HAVE DONE!' She screeched demonically. Joshua reacted with quick pace and grabbed the lamp from the bedside table and threw it right at her face. She disappeared before it hit but that was good enough for Joshua to help Alex out of bed and over to the hatch. Alex began to climb the ladder to the hatch but he was in so much pain that he could not go very fast.

'It's okay Alex, we're getting out of here. We've got to go. You can do it.' Joshua encouraged and helped push Alex upwards. Joshua turned to see the girl had now reappeared at the other end of the room. She made her way towards a now frantic Joshua who desperately tried to help Alex up the ladder. Alex now reached the top of the ladder and fumbled to unscrew the hatch. The girl approached closer and closer. Joshua was dripping with sweat and became ever more restless. Alex opened the hatch and scrambled out as quick as he could. He grabbed Joshua's arm and helped to pull him out but the girl climbed the ladder and began pulling him down.

'Let me go Alex. I did this to her. I need to face her head on. I love you.' Joshua cried. He let go of Alex's hand and allowed himself to be dragged down into the bunker by the girl. Alex cried and called out for Joshua to come back. His heart snapped in two. The hatch to the bunker unexpectedly closed and Joshua's muffled screams soon ceased into silence. Alex collapsed in a heap on the floor and cried his broken heart out.

After six hours of crying and wallowing. Alex opened the hatch and climbed down in the bunker to find Joshua's body slung and broken on the floor. He knelt down and placed Joshua's head in his hands and kissed him on the forehead. He gazed over to the wall of the bunker to see another scratched note on the metal.

'Thank you. Your sacrifice has set me free.' Alex let out an agonising scream that echoed throughout the bunker and collapsed by Joshua's side.

THE HANGING MAN

I always woke up really early in the morning when it was the summer holidays. My mum kicked me out of the house every morning to go and play. I never told her that I didn't have any friends. The other kids at school picked on me a lot. They said I was weird. They pushed me a lot. One boy, Daniel, steals my packed lunch. I never tell my mum about the other boys bullying me because she worries a lot. I can hear her crying in her bedroom at night. I knew she was sad and didn't want to make her worse. I tried to just make her happy.

I ran out of the house as quick as I could to get to the stream in the woods. It was my favourite place to go. Nobody ever went to the stream. Not the bit I went to. That's why I liked it. I headed down the street and through the gate at the start of the woods before venturing to my favourite spot by the creek. I liked picking up pebbles and building a small dam along the creek. I saw a couple of Salamanders every now and again. I picked them up and played with them until they wanted to leave. They were the only friends I needed.

Something was different today. I could see a dark shape near my favourite spot. Nobody came to my spot. Ever. Why was someone in my spot? I crept up to my spot and could see a man in a grey suit. Just standing. I started to feel scared. I didn't talk to the people I knew best. Never mind a stranger. The closer I got to him, I realised that he was not standing. He was hanging. It looked fun. He had a rope around his neck and he dangled off the ground. He must have gotten stuck while playing on his rope. I'd like to play with his rope also.

I was not scared anymore. I went to my usual spot and sat down and began building a small dam. I looked around at the hanging man. He didn't move or speak to me. I liked that. I didn't like to talk to people. I played in the creek and offered the hanging man to come and join me. He didn't say anything so I continued my playing. When the sun began to go down I said goodbye to the hanging man and went home.

My mum was crying on the dining room table when I got in. She had prepared chicken dinosaurs and beans for my tea which I ate quietly. She had her head in her hands and an empty glass of red wine on the table. I decided not to tell her about my new friend because she was upset and went upstairs to bed. My mum didn't always used to be this sad. She started crying a lot recently. Whenever she cried when I was little my dad would make her happy again. I hadn't seen my dad in a while. My mum had a lot of bruises because she was very clumsy. That was why dad had moved into work, because mum was very clumsy. That was why my mum didn't stop crying. He must be working really hard.

In the morning I got up quickly and ran to the creek again. The hanging man was there already. He was still playing with his rope. I said good morning to him but he didn't reply. I liked him a lot. He was my best friend. There were flies landing on the hanging man's face. They really seemed to like him. He was grey and dull looking. His hair was messy and his suit was dirty. He didn't care. He was having fun with his rope. I stood up from the creek and went over to the hanging man. He was cold to touch and his skin felt funny. I asked if I could play with his rope but he didn't answer me. I climbed the tree and untied the rope so I could play with it. He fell to the floor which made me laugh because he was funny. I took the rope off his neck and began to play with it. The hanging man lay on the floor and didn't move. He must be sad. My mum was very still when she was sad. I felt sorry for him so I pulled him over to the creek and sat him up so he could build a dam and play with the Salamanders.

The sun began to set and I said goodbye to the hanging man and went home to my mum who was crying again. Every day for the rest of the summer I got up early, went to the creek and the hanging man and I would play until the sun went down. He always got there before me and left after I did. His mum must have been really nice to let him play out for so long. We would switch between playing with the dam and the water to playing with the rope. I had never had so much fun. The hanging man was my best friend. Every night I came home and my mum cried with a glass of wine. I wish I could make her happy.

I told my mum one night about the hanging man. She looked up from her hands at me. It was the first time I'd seen her face in a long time. She looked angry. She stood up from the table and put her hands on the sink.

'I'd like to meet this friend of yours. He seems to make you very happy.' She said as she grabbed really hard on the sink. I was so excited for my mum to meet the hanging man. She would love him. He was my best friend.

The next day I shot out of bed and I told my mum I was going to bring the hanging man home. She was stood in the kitchen with something in her hands and tears running down her face. I ran as fast as I could to the creek. The hanging man was there before me. He was very skinny now. I told him about meeting my mum but he didn't follow me as I made my way home. I went back and grabbed him and began to pull him home with me. He was very funny the hanging man. I really liked him. We arrived at my house and I went into the kitchen to show my mum.

'Look hanging man! My mum is hanging just like you!'

A STRANGE
APPETITE

I don't like the taste of real food. It repulses me. Naturally, I still eat it to stay alive. What an unfortunate situation. My family and friends tell me I'm too thin and pale. Well, just family. I don't really have any friends. The Doctor told me I'm malnourished. They all tell me to eat more but that isn't going to happen. I look in the mirror and see a stick thin whiter than white person. Barely recognisable as a person. My hair has fallen out from my poor diet and only small tufts remain. I slouch because I am not physically able to stand up straight. Two black rings lay permanently around my eyes. Every single rib is visible, even through my clothes. I am not how I wish to appear but I am how I appear as a result of my dietary affliction.

I finally discovered something two years back. My true addiction. I cut my finger on a nail and put it in my mouth to stop the bleeding. There it was. The metallic tinge ignited life into my bones. Blood. The taste was divine. Far better than any of the mundane garbage people ingest for fun. This was something I could stomach.

After a while, I could not sustain my diet of drinking from myself. I still ate other food to survive but after I discovered the powerful taste I began to eat less and less real food. My health deteriorated fast. I could still sustain my life. I needed another way to get blood. Naturally, I decided to set up a blood bank. I didn't let my parents find out so I stole money from my dad's wallet and bought a storage container to do it from. I advertised on the dark web for the weirdos who would willingly donate money for me to drink. I couldn't falsely advertise that it was for medical purposes, that was morally wrong. To my surprise, I received many donors. I was in paradise. Euphoria swept my person and brought me back from my almost dead state. I drank and drank and drank and never ran out because of the strangeness of the people of the world. Thank you strange people.

Back to now and my blood bank is deteriorating rapidly. The weird people who were willing to donate never came back to donate again and I had a very small pool of donors remaining. My health was back at where it used to be again because not only was I running low on blood, I was still eating enough food to sustain myself. My parents became increasingly concerned for my well-being but I refused to go back to the doctor again.

Two weeks later. My blood bank has run dry. I have no blood to sustain myself for much longer. I need to resort to taking more serious action. In my head I had four options. The first was to do nothing and most likely die. The second, to start to kill people for their blood. That option was automatically out. The third, to snoop around a hospital and see what I could find. That option did not appeal to my morals either. The fourth, was to flee town and move somewhere else where there were donors. This option again seemed unfeasible because I did not have an income, a house, anything. I would not be able to sustain my life without my parents.

Side note: I hate vampire films. The glorification and sexualisation of my condition offended me highly. The male vampires were always extremely ripped and healthy. They were always strong and capable. The women were always also physically fit and able to do so many things. No cinematic vampire is ever dishevelled like me. None of them are weak and cannot survive off blood alone like me. They all still had hair. They had friends. They had everything that I didn't and were still able to go around killing people. I was a true vampire. It is not as easy in real life. I also can't turn into a bat. However I can go out in the sunlight without burning or sparkling, which I suppose is a good thing.

The last of my supply of blood trickled down my throat and I began to seriously panic about my wellbeing. I didn't know what I was going to do. I heard a rattle at the door of my storage container. My heart sank. Probably somewhere visible. Someone is trying to get into my blood bank. Who knows what would happen if anyone found this place? I would be treated like I'm insane. I'm not insane. I haven't hurt anyone, I'm just trying to survive. The door swung open and two police officers stepped in.

'We're going to need you to come with us please.' One of them began to say calmly. All I could think to do was cry.

This wasn't supposed to happen. I was a good person. I killed nobody. I didn't do anything. One of the police officers grabs me by the arm and begins to escort me out.

'Your parents are concerned about you. We need you to come with us and we can get you better. Don't worry you aren't going to prison. We're taking you somewhere where you can get better. Okay?' The officer is friendly enough but I know where they are taking me. I don't want to go to a hospital. I'm a good person. I'm just trying to survive. I don't want to go. I didn't hurt anyone. I had never hurt anyone. I never would hurt anyone. I don't want to go. I don't want to go. I don't want to go. I kick and scream with the little strength I have left. It isn't nowhere near enough to break free of the officers. I can't stop crying and wailing. I'm only fourteen.

LONDON TOWN

I was married on the 16th of January 1864. My husband's name was William, he was a printer's machinist, he was responsible for maintaining and working on the printing press. We had five children, Edward, Percy, Alice, Eliza, and Henry. Things were going well. We enjoyed our time together. He looked after me right. He was a real gentleman. Brought home plenty of money too. We weren't well off but we had enough to get us through. I knew he was having an affair on the nurse who birthed my last child. I wasn't daft. I loved him nonetheless. My father wasn't having any of it. He thought that our relationship ended because of it. He gave him so much grief he did. It was all lies though. We never broke up. 'Course we didn't, I loved him. My father needed to keep his nose out of other people's business.

The affair took its toll on me though. Cause he was having an affair, I went out and made a little extra bit of cash on the side if you know what I mean. I didn't go with no scruffs. I only went with the rich fellas who were willing to pay up. I did it cause I never felt loved at home anymore. It made me feel good about myself and it made cash so I didn't see no problem with it. I could afford a good drink down the pub. Maybe I had too many cause I never went home. I couldn't bear to be around him anymore. He made me sick. I stayed out all night in the pub and worked the corner for a couple of hours. He said I deserted him. We separated not long after. He says it was cause of my drinking.

The police said he still had to support me after we split up cause I didn't have a proper job. 5 shillings a week I got from him. Not bad money. I still worked the streets on a night for a couple extra bob to go down the pub with. Things got complicated in 1882 when he stopped giving me the money cause of my work from the streets. I spent the next few years shifting from workhouse to workhouse, boarding house to boarding house. Never found the right place for me. I never earned the money to get a place of my own. People would give me a bit every now and again and my street work would give me small bits but it was never enough. I moved in with my father for a year cause I was desperate and had nowhere left to go. We got on for most of the year. It was nice to have a place that was stable. I was tired of moving from here to there all the time.

One day, father came home and he started having a go at me. Really angry. I didn't know what to do with myself. I was scared. He started going off because I lived with a blacksmith. He was called Drew and he was one of my clients. My father wasn't having it. He hated me living with another man outside of marriage. It was improper. He called me a tramp among other names and that's when I had it. I moved out as soon as he started having a go. I didn't need to be told I was dirt. Back to moving from house to house. I ran out of money quite fast. I had to now sleep rough. My back was in pain all of the time from my poor diet and sleeping rough. I still worked the streets during the night but had to find somewhere to sleep most of the time. In early 1888 I was sleeping in Trafalgar Square when I was found by someone from the Lambeth Workhouse. They took me in and I lived there for quite a few months.

I left in May cause I found a job. I was a domestic servant. I hated working there. I loved a good drink but the family I worked for never touched the stuff. They had a go at me for my drinking so I had enough. Nobody tells me not to drink. I quit and made off with their fancy clothes. They never used them. They went to waste in their wardrobes. Worth three pounds ten shillings they were. Got me a few good nights down the pub they did. I got a new room, in a common lodging house in Spitalfields. I had a roommate too. Nelly her name is. Nice girl. We got along alright. I was never in much.

It was about half passed 12 on the 31st of August. I was in my new local pub. The Ten Bells it was called. I had a few drinks. I needed to make the money for the bed for the night. I left the pub to go find some business. They turned me out of my bed cause I never had my fourpence. So I told 'em I'd have the money. I just got myself a new bonnet that would help me out. Nobody would want to turn me down with it. I kept going out and making my money. 'Cept every time I did I just went back to the pub and spent it. I saw Nelly while I was waiting for business. I told her I made my bed money three times over but spent it all on booze. She went home and told me to get my money sorted as soon as I could. I never went back to the pub.

A smart gentleman greeted me politely and tipped his top hat. I thought he seemed nice so I decided to go with him. We went a couple blocks down and he agreed to give me the fourpence I needed to get my bed for the night. He was a right gentleman he was. Beautiful man. We went a couple of blocks down to get to business. I knew my new bonnet would get me money. I lifted my skirt and waited for him to have at it. He wasn't doing anything so I shouted him to get a move on. I heard something like metal Ching behind me. I turned around and there he was with a blade in my face. He sliced the blade through my throat twice. I died immediately. He moved my body to a gated stable entrance in Buck's Row. He then had at my stomach. He made several cuts across my stomach and down my side. I never bled much because I was already dead. They found my body at 3:40 am on the 31st of August 1888. My name is Mary Ann Nichols. I am the first victim of Jack the Ripper.

HIDE AND SEEK

It was a beautiful summer's day. Our mums had sent us all out to play all day. We all went up to the church at the top of the hill because it had a huge grassy area around it and a forest so we could play in it. I loved the summer. It was the best time of year. No school and we got to play outside all day. We had no homework or lessons or anything. It was so much fun. We would go out really early every morning and come home really late at night. It was nearly bedtime when we got home.

There were seven of us all together. There was me, my name is Lucas, there was Rebecca, that was my best friend, there was Josh, Priya, Sam, David, and Alison. They were all in my class at school. We played together in school too. They were all my best friends, but Rebecca was my favourite. We hadn't been friends for very long. I had to make new friends after all of my friends moved away. Mum says they had moved to heaven because a bad man was trying to get them. I was sad. I liked them but my new friends were just as nice.

'What are we going to play today?' Priya asked us once we got to the grass. Priya was like a teacher. She liked to boss us around and tell us what to do. At least she didn't give us homework to do.

'Let's play tig!' Josh shouted at her, he was very excited. His favourite game was tig. He wanted to play it every day. Josh was always very excited and full of energy.

'We always play tig! Let's play something different today.' Said Alison. She was always moody. Especially with Josh. My mum says it's because she fancies him. I think she just doesn't like him.

'Let's play bulldog!' David shouted. He was always very good at bulldog because he was very wide and very strong. He liked to play football a lot.

'No you play bulldog really rough!' Sam pushed him. Sam was the leader of the group. He liked to push the boys and be mean to the girls. My mum said he was a bully and didn't like us playing with him but he had no other friends. I didn't like Sam.

'Why don't we play hide and seek?' I suggested. It was my favourite game. I played it a lot with my old friends. I hadn't played it with my new friends yet.

'Good idea. Let's play that!' Rebecca said excitedly. 'Lucas you count first and we'll all hide!' I loved that idea. I liked searching for everyone. It's what I did with my old friends too. I counted to 100 and began to search for everybody. The first person I found was Sam. He was hiding behind a bush on the edge of a very steep cliff. I was happy to find him first because he was a bully and I didn't want to spend long looking for him.

'Found you Sam!' I called as I walked over to him. 'Now you've got to stay here while I go find the others. You're not allowed to move.'

'You can't do that! I'm not staying here. It's rubbish!' Sam shouted as he stepped out from the bush.

'You have to. I'll have to make you stay there. It's the rules.' I pleaded. After convincing him to stay there I went to look for someone else. The next person I found was Josh. I could hear him jumping up and down behind the alter of the church. He was crouching behind a statue of the Virgin Mary.

'Found you Josh! Now stay still and stay there!' There was no way he was going to stay there and be still on his own. I needed something to help him. Luckily, I got him to stay there and went to go and find everyone else.

David was easy to spot. He was hiding under the crumbling down house at the edge of the green space. The house used to belong to the priest of the church but they moved out and it got dirty and destroyed.

'Found you David! Stay there!' I shouted.

'I'm hungry! I want my lunch now! Can you hurry up and find everyone else?' He shouted. David was a very big person. I was going to need something very very big to make him stay there while I found the others. I got him to stay and went off to find the girls.

Alison was next. I found her over by the pond. She was hiding in the reeds. That was a very good hiding place. I wonder where Priya and Rebecca were.

'I am not staying here while you go and look. I'm bored of this game. I'm going home Lucas.' She sighed as usual. I found a way to make her stay and went to find Priya and Rebecca. I found Priya hiding behind a very spiky tree. I liked the spiky tree. It was different from the others like me.

'I am the leader you can't tell me to stay here. I need to make sure the others are okay! Now go and find Rebecca!' Priya bossed me around, but like the others I managed to get her to stay while I searched for Rebecca.

I found her! She was running through the trees. I chased after her until I caught her when she tried to climb over a barbed wire fence.

'Lucas! Stay away from me. My hiding place was to stay behind you and watch you so that I'd win. I saw what you did to the others! Please don't hurt me!' She screamed and started crying.

'What do you mean? I only got them to stay so I could find you!' I asked very confused.

'I saw you push Sam over that cliff! I checked him and he's dead. I saw you throw the statue of Mary on top of Josh and crushed him, you kicked down the columns in the house so that it fell down on David, you pushed Alison in the pond and stamped on her in the water until she stopped moving, and I saw you push Priya onto that branch that went right through her stomach! Please. I don't want to be your friend anymore Lucas.' She tried to climb over the fence but her jeans got stuck on the barbed wire.

'I-I just wanted them to stay that's all.' I said as I grabbed a hold of Rebecca. She screamed for help but nobody was there. 'I'm sorry Rebecca. You can't tell on me. That's mean. You were my best friend!' Rebecca soon stopped screaming. I unfastened her body from the barbed wire and pulled her to the centre of the field where we started playing. I brought Sam, David, Josh, Alison, and Priya so that she wasn't lonely. I was going to miss them all. The same thing happened with my last friends. All I wanted was for them to stay. I can't wait to play hide and seek again with my new friends.

A HELLISH TEST

It's hard to provide an accurate description of my current situation. It was as though all of a sudden, I was able to think. I did not remember not being able to think but I do not remember any of my thoughts up until that moment. Around me was black. No, in fact it was darker than black, more empty and dark. I appeared to be in a void surrounded by an endless perimeter of nothing. Could nothing be endless? It seemed so. I did not think it was possible to feel nothing, and yet the absence of feeling and action was abundant. I could do nothing, be nothing, feel nothing. I was nothing. How was I conscious? Was I conscious? An endless stream of thoughts questioning my very existence and morality plagued my mind. If I had a mind, or even existed for that matter. Every thought I conjured lead to several questions arising and leaving me right back where I started off. Wherever that even was.

I had no memory of anything else apart from the vast nothingness that surrounded me. How was it possible for me to not have memories? I was conscious of my existence and I knew that this form of existence was not the correct one. However I did not know what the correct way of living was. I was sure there was more than this, was there? I could not move at all, I did not know if there was anything to move, and eventually realised that there was no point in moving because my surroundings were just empty. There was nowhere to go or nothing to do except just exist in a state 0f wonder at what made me like this and how I could revert back to whatever existence I had before.

The Deprive is the name I gave to my location, as it felt the only way possible to describe it. I was deprived of my ability to do anything other than think. I did not quite understand how I was able to retain the ability to think, and to form sentences in my head. Alternatively, as far as I knew I could have been saying this all out loud without the slightest realisation. I knew what words meant and could speak (or think) rather eloquently despite my ability to be able to do anything else. A sudden jolt pulsed through me and in that moment I began to feel again. I recognised emotions that I had apparently been able to feel in whatever my past existence seemed to have been. I am a human, I knew that much for sure.

A dimly lit cavern appeared around me. I could move. In that moment I suddenly existed again. I remembered everything of how to act and to feel but I just couldn't remember who I was. A small lantern hung on the wall. I rose to my feet to investigate. What was this place? I looked above me and the roof of this cavern had been lined with the ribcage of some giant creature, creating a breath-taking gothic illusion. I made my way down the corridor as my fingers glided the rock for guidance. At the end of the corridor, stood a large wooden door. The door towered above me. I gave it a push and entered inside.

I appeared to be standing in an enormous stone courtroom. An immense bench for a judge stood in the centre of the far end of the room. Either side of the bench stood two granite grotesques. I remembered that they were called grotesques and not gargoyles because gargoyles were statues used for the drainage of water and grotesques were just for appearance. The rooms entirely empty. Not a single soul seemed to exist here. I was entirely alone. At least that's what I thought. The two grotesques suddenly twisted and snapped themselves to life. They crept up to the bench their eyes showed nothing but pure evil. They jeered at me amongst themselves.

'Welcome to hell!' One of them hissed. 'You have unfortunately been summoned by the reaper himself. We regret to inform you that you did not qualify for heaven because of all of the awful decisions you made in your living years. You are forbidden from having access to any of your memories from your life. You will suffer for an eternity at the hands of our Lord and master, Lucifer!' Both of them howled with laughter.

'Who are you? Is there any way at all I can change things around and go to heaven?' I pleaded. I couldn't go to hell.

'I am Panic.' One of the grotesques announced.

'I am Pain.' The other chimed in.

'There is one way you can get to heaven.' Panic chuckled as he looked at Panic, who also burst into a fit of laughing.

'Anything! I'll do it!' I was desperate. Surely I hadn't been so inhumane in my living years that I was condemned for an eternity of torture.

'There are nine layers of Hell as most people know. This is the first, limbo. If you can face the eight other hellish tests, then you will be granted access to heaven.' Pain chuckled.

'See you soon!' Panic cackled like a witch around a cauldron. They snapped their fingers and like that I wasn't in the courtroom anymore.

I was in a dark space surrounded by nothing except a distant door. I made my way towards the door. It seemed to be miles away. I was suddenly blown back further by an enormous gust of wind. The winds pierced my face. I pushed myself forward, despite the winds blowing me back.

'Welcome to the second circle of hell. Lust. As punishment for people who are consumed by lust, they are blown back and forth by violent winds, which means they are unable to rest. The strong wind symbolises the restlessness of the person consumed by lust.' Pain's voice rang through my ear. I pushed forwards and allowed myself to move. The wind pushed me backward. I ached with pain. The strength it took to push myself forward was overwhelming. I was getting closer. Closer by the second. I stretched out my arm towards the door and pushed myself through.

The third circle of hell was gluttony. I was submerged in a pool of disgusting liquid that had a constant refilling of icy rain above me. The liquid represented the degradation of a glutton who is obsessed with food and drink and the inability to see through the slush represents the selfish neglect of others around the glutton. The icy rain represented the coldness of the glutton for ignoring those around them. The fourth circle represented greed. I was forced to joust against another version of myself using extremely weighted weapons which I had to push with my chest to represent the selfish drive for fortune during lifetime.

I was transported via boat down the river Styx for my next trial. This was the fifth circle of hell and it represented anger. A hoard of skeletons and demons stood on the banks of the fiery river watching as I was transported through. The boat stopped suddenly, I jolted backwards and nearly lost my footing. I was in so much pain. Every joint and muscle of my body throbbed with pain. The boat rocked as a skeletal hand latched itself onto the side of the boat. It layered aboard. I had been instructed that the punishment for anger was to battle to the death on the river. I fought the skeleton with everything I had and knocked it back into the river where it was deemed defeated. Before I could celebrate I was surrounded by a sea of skeletons all clambering onto the small boat. I punched and kicked them as hard as I could. I was given no weapon. They came at me all at once. It was too much for me. I was never going to heaven. I was too exhausted.

Deep down within me, a small fire began to burn. I stood up proud and fought like a warrior. I couldn't live my life in torture. I needed to complete the trials. I fought and fought until I was the only one standing. I had done it. I was ready to move to the next circle. For the sixth circle I was enclosed in a flaming tomb from which I had to escape. The punishment was for heresy. The seventh circle was by far the worst. It was a representation of violence. The first test within the circle was being sunk in a river of boiling blood and fire, which was the intended punishment for murderers. I was then turned into a tree where I was fed upon by harpies, which was how people who committed suicide were punished. I was chased and ripped to shreds by a pack of ravenous wolves. In the final ring, for sodomites, I was trapped in a desert that rained fire and had to find a way to escape. I made it to the eight circle. The fraudulent were trapped in various caverns and hunted down by Geryon, a flying monster who adapted different natures to represent the many natures of the fraudulent.

I was so close to an afterlife of paradise. It felt like many years since I first started my venture through the circles of hell. The final circle was for the treacherous. I was enclosed in an icy lake and must make my escape. I contemplated how I would make my escape from the ice. I was entirely enclosed. My entire body was numb and raw. I had been severely injured from every stage of my adventure. I was so weak. I forced movement in my hands. I forced through a millimetre of ice. Scratching one millimetre at a time. Scratch. Scratch. Scratch. This truly was torturous. What felt like years passed me by and I still worked away at the ice. An eternity had gone by and I nearly had made it to the surface. My fingers had worn down to the bone. Another eternity passed. I'd done it. I was free. I had escaped at long last. Panic and Pain returned me to the courtroom after my trials.

'Can I please go to heaven now?' I pleaded. They looked at each other and laughed.

'Nobody can just switch from hell to heaven. We've been playing you. There is no way you can ever get to heaven now. You're doomed for eternity. It was fun to watch though.' They cackled at me as I sunk to the floor and cried.

THE HOUSE ON LINFORD GREEN

Abigail Morrister looked at herself in the mirror as she waited for her parents to return. She had heard the car pulling up the drive and ran downstairs to greet them. She saw her father, Louis, against the mosaic glass in the door. She greeted him with a hug and waited for her mother, Jennifer, to enter. She ran to her mother's arms who scooped her up into her arms and carried her through to the kitchen. Abigail was always scared being left in the house on her own. The servants always went missing and she was completely alone in the seemingly infinite mansion.

The Morrister mansion lay on top of a small hill in the forest of Linford Green. It was a typical woodland mansion. Iron gates leading to a long driveway, ivy rising above the main entrance, grey stone making up the exterior, the works. The Morrister's had inherited it from Jennifer's parents when they died four years ago. They made their money centuries ago and kept it in the family for generations to come.

While Jennifer and Louis unpacked, Abigail played in the garden while the maid, Patrice, took down the washing. She played with her dolls as a cold breeze and grey clouds took shape above her head. Patrice was a frail old woman that often scared Abigail. She had two different coloured eyes, one white, one blue. She had been in the family for decades.

'He's going to get you, you know.' She croaked at Abigail. She looked up from her dolls and pondered what she could have meant. She ignored her and continued playing.

'He's coming for you.' Patrice sang as she shuffled closer. 'He's always watching you. Just look, over there, in the woods. Can you see him?' Abigail looked at where Patrice was pointing and saw an extremely tall and broad dark shadow shuffling through the trees. It was running from her vision. It did not want to be seen. She had never seen a man so tall before. She felt the tears coming and ran into the house to be comforted by her mother. Patrice cackled and gazed off into the woods.

'Your time will come. It will come.' She staggered her way into the house with the box of washing.

Later that evening, the sun had begun to set and as Abigail played with her dolls outside again. Jennifer was standing in the kitchen and Louis was upstairs in his study. Jennifer stared out of the window into the back garden before smiling lovingly at Abigail playing. To her horror, she looked up from Abigail to see a dark shape standing at the edge of the woods.

It was a man. A tall and broad man. She could not make out any features she could just see a black shape and that was enough to send shivers down her spine. Their land was entirely closed off by a 10 foot fence.

'Abigail! Come in please! Right now!' She ran outside and grabbed Abigail and dragged her into the house, eyes fixated by the dark figure. She felt sick. She could not act on that right now; her motherly instincts had kicked in and she needed to protect her baby at all costs. Jennifer locked the kitchen door and grabbed the phone to call the police.

'Louis!' She said as he entered the kitchen. 'Check the camera to see if the gate is closed.' She was frantic at this point.

'It is yes. Why?' Louis inquired, placing his hands on Abigail's head to comfort her.

'Hello. Police please. There is someone trespassing on our land and watching my child. I live at Morrister Manor in Linford Green. Thank you. Bye.' She put the phone down and clutched her pearls as she turned to Louis.

'What? I'm going out there. Nobody goes near my baby girl.' Louis cried as he burst through the door. He was grabbed by Patrice as he was leaving the door.

'Don't worry Mr. Morrister. I'm so sorry. I forgot to tell you. That's my son. He came to visit me in my summer house on the land. I was going to introduce him to you but he's very shy you see. I'm so sorry to cause all of this fuss. I'm ever so sorry.' Patrice flustered as she placed her hands on her head.

'Don't worry Patrice. Everyone makes mistakes. It just startled us is all.' Jennifer said as she placed her hands on

Patrice's shoulders and rubbed them to comfort her. Patrice grinned at Abigail and placed her index finger to her lips. As they were heading inside, Patrice whispered in Abigail's ear.

'That was easy. He's still going to get you.' Abigail looked off into the woods to see the shadow man standing there. She could just see his green eyes. Unblinking. Unsettling.

The next day, Abigail was playing by the edge of the woods while Jennifer sat on the deck and relaxed. Patrice whispered something to Jennifer and she headed back inside the house. Abigail did not notice this but she did notice a small rustling in the trees. She was scared of the shadow man so began to collect her dolls and head back to the house. As she picked up her last doll she noticed a set of black boots walking towards her eyeline. She left her dolls and made a run for the house, locking the door when she got inside. Patrice noticed her return and pursed her lips in disappointment.

Jennifer put Abigail to bed and read her a story. Abigail's bedroom had a balcony and was situated on the first floor facing the back of the house. Abigail fell asleep and Jennifer went to bed herself. A few hours into the night, Abigail felt something strange and jolted awake. She gazed around her room to find a rainstorm outside her window through her thin linen curtains. As she was about to head back to sleep a bolt of lightning illuminated the balcony. She froze. Petrified. The lightning had not only illuminated the balcony, but that of an extremely tall, dark figure standing on her balcony. She could not move. She tried to scream but only a raspy whisper was able to leave her body.

Abigail pulled her duvet up to right underneath her eyes, which she kept fixated on the balcony. A hand pressed itself against the glass door, splattered with rain. The doors pushed open and she could see him emerge through her curtains. He approached the bed so gently, so carefully, so quietly. She shuddered and repeatedly tried to move or call for help but she could not. He reached out his hand to grab her. He was stood right beside her. Reaching right for her face.

Abigail closed her eyes as the shadow man reached out his hand towards her face. She could move. Adrenaline surged through her body and she lunged at the shadow man, knocking him back and ran out of her room, shouting for her parents help. Louis and Jennifer exited their rooms as quickly as they could.

'Are you okay? What's happened my love?' Jennifer screamed as she embraced her child with her protective arms.

'The man from the woods. He's in my room! He tried to get me!' Abigail sobbed as she hugged her mother back.

'What? Let me get him!' Louis stormed through to the bedroom and inspected it to find nothing there. The doors to the balcony were closed. Her wardrobe was empty. Nobody was underneath her bed or in any nook or cranny there was.

'Honey, there's nobody here don't worry. You just had a nightmare that's all. I know what happened earlier was scary but there's nobody here that will hurt you. It was just a mistake is all. I bet this storm isn't helping you either is it? Do you want to come and sleep with us?' Jennifer calmly suggested, taking her little girl's hand and walking her towards the master bedroom. Abigail caught a glimpse of Patrice glaring at her from the end of the corridor. Behind her, a tall and broad shape slunk away into the shadows.

The next day, Abigail was again playing outside in the garden with her dolls. She put her dolls down as she went inside to get a glass of water. It was a very hot summer day. Jennifer bathed in the sun's rays around the other side of the house. Abigail returned to her dolls to find herself feeling fearful and scared. She looked down and her favourite doll, a blonde barbie doll, to see that her hair had been ripped from her head and a pair of scissors had been lodged into her chest, dripping with red goo. She screamed for help and ran into the house and locked the door. She frantically gazed around the edge of the woods to see a dark shape moving back into the shadows.

She backed away from the window slowly towards the kitchen door. She bumped something hard. She clenched her fists and turned around slowly to find a huge man standing right in behind her. It was the shadow man. Abigail screamed louder and ran as quickly as she could to the back door to fumble around with the lock. The shadow man slowly approached her. She panted and sweat as her damp hands slipped across the lock. She couldn't get it open. He was right behind her. He clasped his hand around her mouth as she squirmed for freedom.

Abigail was petrified. Nothing she could do broke her free from his heavy grasp. She kicked and wriggled but she could not break free. He grasped harder and harder. She began to feel weak. The only thing she could think to do was to bite down on his hand. Hard. He yelled in pain and let go of her, allowing her to run to the front door and escape. Abigail was relieved. She was free. She immediately ran over to her mother and explained what had happened.

'What! Are you okay? Let me go and find him.' Jennifer said as she rose from her deck chair and made her way back into the house. She checked every room but found nobody there. Abigail insisted that he was there and went to show her the barbie doll.

'Oh my gosh! Abigail go to your room right now! How dare you do this to something your father and I spent money on! We buy you these things for you to treat them carefully and to play with them properly! Not vandalise them!' Jennifer had never shouted at Abigail like that before. She could tell it had really sent a shiver down her daughter's spine. Patrice made her way over to the pair with an icy glare fixed on Abigail.

'I'm so sorry! My son saw what your daughter did to her barbie doll and tried to calm her down and ask her why she had vandalised it. He must have startled her. He isn't the most social person I'm so sorry Jen.' She delicately apologised. Placing a comforting hand on Jennifer's arm.

'Don't touch me! How dare your son attempt to discipline MY daughter. That's down to me and her father. Not you and your son. Oh and by the way, I find it extremely unprofessional you invite your son to stay on OUR land without our permission. We haven't even met him and you think he has some sort of authority to discipline our daughter? Who the hell do you think you are? Get your stuff. You're fired!' Jennifer screamed mercilessly at Patrice. Who seemed disheartened. She staggered over to her house and gave one final glare to Abigail.

That night, Jennifer and Louis were attending the theatre together and needed to hire a babysitter to look after Abigail after what had happened with Patrice. She arrived a little after six. She was a young girl, named Abbie, which she tried to use to bond with Abigail, unsuccessfully. Abigail put herself to bed and ignored Abbie the entire night. At around eleven she was woken by the creak of her bedroom door. She gazed over in the darkness and allowed her eyes to adjust to see Patrice standing there with an evil grin on her face.

'Hello Abigail. We have some unfinished business.' She prodded over to the bed and grabbed Abigail by the arm and started dragging her to the door. Abigail screamed and tried to break free.

'Scream all you want girl. Nobody is coming for you. I told your little babysitter to go home early as I was here to look after you. Your parents will be back soon and there's something I want you to see.'

'Get off me! I don't want to see it. I don't like you. You're evil and scary!' Said Abigail as she scratched Patrice's hand to try and get her to free her. This did not work and Patrice dragged her harder, pulling her shoulder socket a little too hard. Abigail called out in pain, despite knowing there was nobody that could save her. Patrice dragged her to the front door, opening it to allow her to see out of it. She saw the shadow man standing by the trees next to the driveway. A set of headlights appeared in the distance which made Abigail elated. Her parents had come to save her. At last.

She called out to them but Patrice silenced her. As the car approached the house, the shadow man pushed a nearby tree right onto the road, causing Abigail's parent's car to swerve off the road. They attempted to brake but couldn't under the slippery mud of the forest. Abigail watched in horror as her parents slid at full speed into a large ditch in the woods smashing their windshield on the rocky edge of the ditch and practically destroying the car. Abigail broke free of Patrice and ran to the edge of the ditch to see her parents still moving and attempting to escape. The shadow man stood on the other side of the ditch, bathed in darkness. He shuffled himself behind a tree and pushed the tree, that he had cut earlier in preparation, causing it to crash down on top of the car, completely crushing the roof and Bonnet under its weight. He glared at Abigail and began to make his way across the ditch to grab her.

Abigail stumbled through the woods in an attempt to escape the shadow man's grasp. She was petrified. She could not yet process the death of her parents but her emotions were trying to force themselves out. She neared the gate at the front of the land. It was locked. She pushed and pulled to force the gates open but they would not budge. She panicked greatly. Off in the distance, she could see the shadow man slowly approaching her. He was getting ever closer. She needed an escape. Fast.

She lodged her foot on one of the bottom rungs of the iron gates and began to make her ascent up the gate. She climbed higher. She was nearly at the top now. The shadow man loomed around the bottom of the gate like a hungry predator waiting for its prey. Waiting ever so eagerly for the prey to make a slip up and fall. Right into his grasp. She could feel her thighs weakening as she used every last bit of her energy to hoist herself to the top of the gate. Her breathing was heavy and lumbering. One wrong foot. That's all it was. She thought the next rung was lower than it actually was. Abigail tumbled to the ground and right into the grasp of the shadow man. Horrified was not a strong enough word to describe what she was feeling.

'You thought you could honestly escape?' A familiar voice croaked in Abigail's ear. Patrice stepped out of the shadows and joined the shadow man. She glared down at Abigail with pure hatred in her eyes. The pair dragged Abigail to her feet and forced her to come with them. They walked through the woods back up to the house and over to the cabin where Patrice lived.

'I bet you're wondering what we're planning to do with you. Aren't you?' Patrice snapped as she pushed Abigail into the house. 'Don't worry we aren't going to kill you. We didn't mean to kill your parents but they got in the way.' The shadow man opened a rotted wooden door leading to a pitch black staircase of which there seemed to be no end. The pair began to lead Abigail down into the basement, her trembling hands clutched in fear.

'This isn't about you really.' Patrice began. 'Things have been hard for me and my son, you see. We don't have too much money at the minute. Times are tough. We asked your father if he could give me a pay raise but he simply refused. I needed to do something fast. So, I asked my son to come and help me devise a plan. He began watching you all and wondering the best way to get money out of your family. We couldn't steal from you. Your parents would have fired me there and then.' She paused as they reached the bottom of the stairs. Inside the room, there was a small wooden chair with walls padded with foam.

'One day, we finally realised the perfect plan. I always resented you. Little brat. I had so much more time to myself when I didn't have a snivelling child in my care. I wanted rid of you so badly. That's when it hit me. The government and the police gave millions and millions of pounds to fund the disappearances of children. If I became a figurehead along with your parents in your disappearance, I would get a decent share to get me out of my troubles.' The shadow man dragged a crying Abigail over to the wooden chair and forced her to sit before tying her arms and legs and taping her mouth shut.

'Of course, you're a lot more slippery than you seem. We could never manage to actually get you in our grasp. Then when your mother fired me, our plan blew up in our faces. I couldn't be the heartbroken face of a missing child case now, I'd be the prime suspect. That's when we decided they had to go. The headlines would be perfect. Housekeeper devastated after parents of now missing eight year old Abigail Morrister are brutally murdered. She pleads for anyone to give any information they may have relating to the case and is desperate for donations to pursue the investigation. The pay-out would be far more for me than if your parents were in the picture. It all worked out so perfectly.' She let out a witchy cackle and made her way over to the door.

'Have fun down here Abigail. Don't worry, you will be released in a couple of years when the investigation runs dry and I will be the hero who finds you. We'll drop food down through a small hatch hidden under my carpet and my son will pop down to feed you. Oh, and as for this suspicious looking wooden door leading to a strange dark basement, as of tomorrow it will no longer exist. My son and I are re-plastering the walls. We need a fresh look. The cabin is looking a little drab. That's when I'll stumble over to the house only to find poor mummy and daddy DEAD in their car and phone the police in a state of panic. Toodles.' She ascended the stairs with the shadow man and slammed the door shut, locking it after her. Abigail sobbed quietly as she remained in darkness.

As the hours passed, Abigail wriggled her arms to break free of the ropes. She struggled and struggled but it was no use, she was just making herself weaker. At a little after dawn, the shadow man descended through the ceiling hatch with food on a small tray descending after him. He untied Abigail's mouth so that she could eat. He fed her the slop from the tray as she cried. All of a sudden, the shadow man was landed with such a large slap right across his face. He was taken aback as Abigail jumped from the chair and smashed the food tray right across his face, knocking him unconsciousness. Little had he known that she had in fact been successful in untying herself during the night.

She climbed the rope that the tray had entered from and was free. Patrice was nowhere to be seen in the dank shack. She must have headed over to call the police. Abigail knew she needed to stop her. She knew she needed to be exposed for what she had done. She marched over to her house, being wary of Patrice and the danger she possessed. The house was completely empty. She was nowhere to be seen. She had not called the police yet Abigail could tell. She grabbed herself a knife from the kitchen to protect herself if anything happened.

As Abigail crept around the house, she did not notice Patrice lurking behind her, ever so quietly, with a metal bar raised to attack. Abigail ascended the stairs to her bedroom, Patrice following close behind her. A creak on the floorboards alerted Abigail to duck out of the way as the metal bar swung at her and nearly hit her. It smashed into the door frame and Patrice struggled to free it. While Patrice struggled with the metal bar, Abigail ran at her with the knife. She ducked just in time and freed the metal bar. It flew across the room and narrowly missed Abigail. Patrice lunged at Abigail in frustration. She reacted quickly and dodged out of the way, spun around, and dragged the knife right into Patrice's back. A glass shattering howl escaped Patrice's mouth as she tumbled to the floor in a heap, unmoving, still. Abigail watched for a second as Patrice lay silently on the floor. In floods of tears, she headed downstairs and called the police.

DREAM BOY

I was in school. Except, it wasn't like school. Things were different. The objects all began to move. They were all misshapen and askew. I walked the psychedelic corridors that seemed to stretch for an eternity. The lights were off and I could not seem to find a switch to turn them on. The school was basked in an eerie green light that seemed to radiate from nowhere and everywhere at the same time. I scaled the corridors that seemed to resemble Relativity by M.C Escher. The shadows danced like sprites. They played awful tricks on my mind, making me believe I was seeing the supernatural.

One corridor hosted a strange black lump on the floor. I watched at the opposite end for my own safety. The lump began to form a shape. I knew it must be the shadows and their tricks again but I couldn't tear myself away. The shape grew legs, four of them, as black as the night itself, a tail, as long as its legs, covered in thick black fur, two long raggedy ears, and a long snarling snout. It was a large dog. A dog with dirty fur and a rabid look in its eye. I had always been terrified of dogs ever since I was little. My mum had taken me to the park for the first time. A dog ran over to me, knocked me off my feet, and sunk its teeth right into my arm. Luckily, the dog had to be put down, but that had never eased my fear of them.

The hound growled at me and bared his teeth. He hunched forwards to signal that he was about to attack. He had a distinctive scar above his left eye, which had turned his fur around that area white. I retreated to the next corridor and began to run. I could hear the thundering clatter of paws behind me. I navigated corridor by corridor. Everyone seeming to be longer than the last. There didn't seem to be any entrances or exits. I was trapped in an infinite loop of corridors. The dog skidded around the corner and smashed its body into the wall of lockers. Thick and sickly slaver escaped his fangs as he charged full speed towards me. I couldn't stop now. I was so tired. When was this corridor going to end?

Finally, I could see something at the end of the corridor. A light. Small but that was enough to give me faith. I ran towards it, the hell hound on my tail. Closer. Closer. The dog also got closer. Closer. I skidded to stop myself. At the end of the corridor was a steep, rocky drop into the abyss. The corridor just came to an end. I stumbled to try and avoid falling to my death. I leaned over the edge and stared into the darkness. The clatter of paws loomed behind me. I turned to face the demon. He glared at me with unloving eyes. I pleaded that it would be over quickly. He took a lunge at me and everything went blank.

I awoke screaming in a pool of sweat. I jolted upright and switched on my light. My nightmares were returning. I hadn't had a nightmare like that in years. I'd stopped taking the pills that my doctor had prescribed lately. I thought that after all of these years it would have gone away. I was wrong.

'What's wrong Charlie?' My mum came in frantic. She wrapped her arms around me and held me tight. 'I told you it might not be for the best to stop taking your pills. Come here.'

'I really thought this time I'd be better. It's been ten years since I was first on them and nothing has changed at all.' I sobbed into my mum's shoulder.

'At least it was only a nightmare this time. Remember how bad things were before?' She stroked my face so gently. The way that mother's know best.

'I know. I'm fifteen now though. I don't want to take dream repressing pills anymore. I should have grown out of it entirely.'

'I know it's sad but that's just the way it has to be. You call me right away if anything like last time happens again. Try and get some sleep and remember to take your pills tomorrow. Good night.'

The next day I arrived at school to my usual beating by the bullies. Craig, Jack, and Bone. Real name. They had bullied me for as long as I can remember. The school did nothing, naturally. They first bullied me when I was five years old. In a nightmare. They then began haunting my every waking moment too. They were the one nightmare my pills couldn't take away. I gave them my dinner money as usual and they proceeded to pick on me. They called me weird and mocked me for wearing glasses. Nothing I'd never heard from them before. I headed out into the yard to find my friends.

I saw something move along the fence outside. The hedges masqueraded the shape at first until it moved into the clear. I was aghast. Thick, black fur, four legs, a tail, two long and tatty ears. A black hound. Not only a black hound, one that had a scar above his left eye that had turned the fur around it white. It was happening again. I ran inside to get away from it. The corridors became a blur. A psychedelic haze with long, winding corridors that seemed to have no end.

'It's happening again mum. I promise I'll take the pills. Please come and get me. I'm scared.' I whimpered down the phone as I locked myself in a toilet cubicle.

"Oh no sweetheart what is it this time?' Mum replied sympathetically.

'A rabid black hound. It's outside the school. Please.'

'I'm on my way, stay calm.' I sobbed in the cubicle in fear.

At the age of five years old, I began to have extremely realistic nightmares about the monster underneath my bed. He would stretch out a furry hand from underneath my bed at night and pull me underneath to my doom. The nightmares occurred every night for four weeks. My mum took me to therapy because it had gotten that bad. Every night I woke up screaming. I lived in fear of the monster under my bed. Things changed one night. The monster reached out his arm as usual. He grabbed me and began to pull me underneath the bed. I screamed and screamed but this time I didn't wake up. The light outside my room flickered on. My mum and dad burst into the room and began to tug me from underneath the bed. They managed to break me free of the monster's grasp and watched in horror as the monster's arm flailed around my room trying to grab me again.

I wasn't dreaming. My nightmare had manifested itself into the real world. My mum tried everything but everyone believed she was insane. Eventually, we found a psychiatrist who claimed to have worked a similar case. He prescribed me dream repressing drugs. I've been taking them ever since. My parents saw the monster first hand and could not deny their own eyes. They saw my dream manifest itself into reality. From that moment they knew that nothing would be normal again.

I arrived home with my mum. When we arrived inside she made me take my pills straight away. I would never stray from using them again. I had a peaceful and undisturbed night of sleep that night. I had no dreams and therefore no nightmares. It was heavenly. I woke the next day and headed to school as normal. I was greeted at the gates of the school by Craig, Jack and Bone. They pushed me over and pulled my underpants to give me a wedgie. They hit me several times and dragged me into the school. The teachers laughed and thought that they were playing. Jack held me up against the lockers while Craig punched my stomach.

I'd had it. After school I knew what I needed to do. I researched all night. Lucid dreaming and how to achieve it. How to actively take control of your dreams and choose what you wanted to dream about. I practiced for the next week. I stopped my medication. Luckily, it had no negative effect on me. while this occurred, I was tortured every single day. They beat me harder each day. My lucid dreaming became easier to control.

On Friday, I felt more confident in myself. I walked into school with a swing in my step. I knew what I was getting myself in for that night. I was greeted at my locker by all three of them. Bone punched my stomach so that I fell against the lockers. Jack grabbed a hold of my shirt and ripped it open, tearing all of the buttons from it. He punched me in the groin. I limped over in pain while the boys stole my shirt and jacket, leaving me standing there topless. Craig pulled a pocket knife from his jacket and used it to slit a hole in my pants, around my bottom. Other children gathered around and laughed at me. They jeered. Mocked. Pointed at me. I wanted to die. No. I wanted to kill them. This solidified my plans for the night even more. I burst out of school and ran home crying. Why wait until tonight? I'll just take a nap now. I was going to kill the three of them. I had not taken my medication and now that I knew how, I was going to manipulate my dream so that all three of them died. I prayed that reality would kick in and follow suit.

I was in the school. The distorted school from before. By my side, as a companion, was the rabid hound. We scoured the corridors together, hunting for my tormentors. Together, nothing could stop us. I looked down at my companion of revenge. He looked up at myself. There they were. At the end of the corridor. They looked up at me. There was a fourth person with them. They seemed to have stabbed them. They were lying on the floor, dead. I ran closer. No longer would anyone be victimised under the tyrannical reign of those bullies. The hound and I approached with valour. A familiar face lay at the foot of the bullies. The valour faded into mourning. It was my mum.

I jumped out of bed and ran into the kitchen. I called and screamed for her but she was nowhere to be found. I ran upstairs to the bedroom and there she was. Lying in a pool of her own blood. My own anger and determination for revenge had blown up in my face. The glory of victory that I should have felt had been replaced with a heartbreak that bares no description. I was in agony. I knelt down beside her and held her head in my hands. A bright light glared through the room. A deep bellowing voice rung through the air.

'Charlie Johnson! Don't worry. This is all a game. You have been a part of a one off TV special, Dream Boy.' I was horrified. My mum rose from the pool of blood and grinned at me. I had no idea what had been going on.

'Four weeks ago, you signed the waver to take part in a new reality TV show. We pitched to you the idea and you agreed to the terms. You will be confused and remember none of this at the moment. We have been conducting psychological and medical experiments on you to make you truly believe that your dreams manifested into life. We implanted artificial memories of the experience occurring in your childhood and gave you several hallucinogenic drugs to induce a seemingly dream-like state in which we introduced the hound. We re-introduced the hound outside your school to complete the effect. Your mum is perfectly fine, that too was another constructed situation. Don't worry everything is fine. You are perfectly safe and will be able to continue life as normal from now on. Thank you for taking part. ' I still didn't understand. My whole life seemed to be a lie. My parents, the bullies, everyone had been in on some elaborate prank to make me believe I had supernatural powers. I wished this was a dream, but deep down I knew it was nothing of the sort.

THE MANY
LIVES OF
ROBERT BROWN

My name is Robert Brown and I can't die. I discovered this many years ago at a summer fair in my local park. It was a sweltering day. The sun gleamed down on the fair-goers, reducing them to slouching piles of sweat. I had always loved this type of weather. I'd take this over winter any day. I was fifteen at the time. I boarded the Ferris wheel with my friends, Jack and Kym. We'd been on every other ride and played every stall, Kym had won a giant teddy bear and Jack had won a Minion stuffed toy that he for some reason kept with him. The Wheel groaned and creaked as we ascended. We thought nothing of it. We reached the top and let out a scream that echoed across the full fair. We could see Kym's house from up here. A screw fell loose on our car and clinked its way down to the ground.

'Oh no. That doesn't look good.' Jack whimpered. He was always scared of anything and everything.

'It's probably nothing.' Kym reassured him. 'These things are so old. Bits fall off them all the time and nobody has ever died. That I know of.'

Jack fidgeted around in his seat and trembled as his hands clutched onto the railings for dear life. This unsettled me and Kym. We tried to calm him down but the more we said seemed to agitate him even more. The cart rocked with Jack's fidgeting. We swayed from side to side in the cart that made the most horrific groaning sound like it was in immense pain. A metallic clang caught the attention of the three of us. One of the clasps fastening the cart to the Wheel had slipped from its place. We were now dangled sideways on the top of the wheel. Jack began to slip from the carriage. Kym and I grabbed onto his arm to try and pull him back in. My grasp was loose from sweating through fear and the heat. Jack slipped away from us so quickly. He plummeted down to the ground, smashing his body against the many metal railings on the descent.

'Hold on! We're sending someone up to come and get you!' A distant voice shouted from below. Kym was the next to slip away. She didn't hit as many bars as Jack but her condition was still fatal. My grip on the cart became weak. I could feel myself falling. My heart sunk a while before I did. Smack. Crash. Crack. I hit every metal beam at full force cracking my head on almost every single one. I crashed to the floor, head first. That should have killed anyone. Broke every bone in their body. The crowd gasped in awe as I rose to my feet, completely unharmed.

The months after the accident were brutal. My memories haunted my every waking moment. The faces of Kym and Jack stained my mind. Their ghosts loomed over me. Why had I survived and they hadn't? I took pills to end my suffering but they had no effect on me. I swallowed more. Still nothing. When I was 18 I was hiking on a clifftop and lost my footing, falling all the way to the bottom and impaling myself on a rock. I slid off the rock and my wound healed immediately.

Ten years later from the accident. I fully came to terms with the fact that I could not be killed. I was married to the love of my life, Lucy. We had no children yet but shared a home together in my childhood town. Everything was going perfectly. She worked in an average office job and I worked as a painter. Our life was normal.

'I cannot stand that bloody man. Drives me up the wall.' Lucy burst through the door one day. She threw her bag and coat down on the floor and poured herself an immense glass of wine. She was speaking of her boss, Ross Hammond. She had always hated him. I comforted her and got her to tell me everything. He'd been giving her unnecessary amounts of work when another colleague was sat around doing nothing.

Later that evening, we went for a walk together. The autumn wind cut our faces as we crunched our way through the mahogany leaves. I held her hand as we smiled and laughed together. We talked about anything and everything. A young man in a hood could be seen crossing to the same side of the road as us further down the street. We thought nothing of it and continued our path. The man approached as I caught a glimmer of something in his pocket. Without a second thought of it, the man lunged a knife right through the centre of my chest, piercing my heart. Lucy screamed and flapped for help as she handed the man her handbag. He pulled his knife from me and proceeded to stab me several times in the chest. Lucy wailed in agony as the man ran away with her purse.

'Oh no. Oh please no.' She sobbed as she approached me. Of course Lucy didn't know that I couldn't die. She was grieving my loss. It broke her heart a little when I explained my condition and the harsh reality that we could never grow old together hit her like a brick. She was distant the full walk home. She walked upstairs to bed and spoke no word to me.

The next day, Lucy burst through the door again in a fit of rage. This time she paid me no mind and ran upstairs, shielding her shirt from my view. A few days later, there was a strange knock at the door. Two police officers stood menacingly on the porch.

'Robert Brown, we are arresting you on suspicion of the murder of Ross Hammond.' The officers announced along with the usual police proceedings. I didn't quite understand at first. It wasn't until I was charged with the murder of Ross Hammond that everything sunk in.

'A life sentence for me means I could die in prison' Lucy explained on one of her conjugal visits. 'You're immortal so a life sentence means nothing to your life span. You do understand right baby? I had to do it. He was a horrible, horrible man. I feel awful for throwing you under the bus but it was the only thing I could think to do. You have so many more years ahead of you. I told the police you'd discovered I was having an affair with Ross and killed him in a fit of rage. I'm sorry Robert. That was the way it had to be. We could never grow old together anyway.'

She was wrong when she said I'd have many more years after serving a life sentence. Life meant life. I had no release date. I've been here for nearly ninety years. The police find nothing strange. They don't even notice I'm here. Day in. Day out. I'm tortured. For something I didn't do. Lucy would be long dead by now but I still plotted my revenge. I would meet her again someday and truly punish her for what she's done to me.

EVERLASTING

I remember every detail of my death. Every second. Every pain. I was young and healthy but that doesn't mean you can escape the ever-looming grasp of death. It was all so sudden. One minute I was exercising every day and had everything together, a loving husband and three beautiful children, and the next I was here. I've been here for around sixty years now. I guess I'm a ghost. A phantom. A poltergeist. To me, the word poltergeist sounds almost offensive. It sounds as though I'm a negative influence. A parasite. I didn't choose to be here, I just was.

After my death, I appeared at the house. A lovely house. Modern, rather large. I was also naturally confused and tried to leave the house to soon discover that I could not. I could not physically step over the door. I tried many different things to escape. Nothing seemed to work. I began to understand how spirits became malicious, not that I would ever be like that. The house was truly luxurious. Every inch was perfectly decorated and kept as tidy as can be. I supposed if I was going to be there for an eternity then it was one of the better places to be trapped.

I soon discovered that I did not need to eat or drink, or even sleep, in fact. I could just exist and wander the grounds of the house and that was the extent of my abilities. This repetitive cycle lasted for four years. Nothing changed. Nobody seemed to live in the house. I was completely alone.

Finally. Something happened. A young woman moved into the house. A beautiful woman. She had auburn hair that glowed in the sunlight, giving her the most angelic beauty I had never witnessed before. She breathed a fresh new aura into the house after years of gloom and loneliness. The house had been a void of happiness until she appeared. She had the softest hazel eyes that were perfectly positioned on her pristinely symmetrical face. I eagerly awaited every day that I would be in the same house as her.

She like to read. Her books were stacked high on the shelves. She read a different one every day. The smile on her face whenever she read one was perfect. It touched my soul to see her so happy. If I had a soul. I think I was only a soul at this point. She had so many books that she had to devote an entire room to them. She built shelf upon shelf upon shelf and converted what was a bedroom into the most beautiful library. She added a white Chaise Lounge so that she could relax and truly indulge herself.

I learned that she had inherited the house from her parents after they died. It was their summer home when she was a child and always longed to return one day. She thought about them every day. She had a framed picture of the three of them that she held in her arms every morning. A couple of times she even shed a tear for them. Every day that I observed her, I fell in love with her even more. Every action she made was so graceful in its own majestic way. She was truly beautiful.

Things began to change one day when she returned home from what I assumed, was a night out with friends, with a man. They entered the house. Tongues locked together. They fumbled around together and eventually entered her bedroom. I did not follow them through because I respected her privacy. I did not observe every single action she made because I respected her more than anything. It irritated me that she was with a man. I know it makes no sense because she was completely unaware of my existence and we could never be together. I tried to ignore my feelings of annoyance.

Over the coming weeks, she began seeing the man more often. He came over more regularly and they developed a close relationship. Every day I felt more disheartened in the house. I had watched her every day for so long and now somebody else had appeared to admire her for her beauty. Every day I felt more like a trespasser. I used to feel welcome when I was alone with her but now things had changed. She had been alone too and I liked to think she was slightly aware of my presence and comforted by it.

Within a year, he had moved in with her. He shared the house with us now. I was still unable to set foot over the door but I tried every single day. Cracks began to form in the relationship. He grew angrier. He often took it out on her. This made me angry in turn because she was an angel fallen from heaven. She did not deserve to be treat so cruelly. He shouted in her face as soon as he got home from work until he went to sleep.

I learned that if I concentrated hard enough, I could move things in the house. This development came through my anger at him one night and a lamp fell off the table and smashed, which caused him to cut his feet. The more I tried, the more I could do. I threw books, cutlery, and ornaments at him over the course of the next couple of weeks. Every time he hurt my precious angel I hurt him in return. The violence between them escalated one winter night when he physically slapped her right across the face. I tried to fend him off by smashing plates in the kitchen and hit him over the head.

He was enraged. He was the devil and she was my angel. He grabbed one of the shards of the plates and lunged at her, cutting her arm. She screamed out for help but there was nobody there to hear her. Except for me. I pushed him back, allowing her to run up the stairs to call the police. He pursued her like a maniac and cut the cord to the phone and pushed her onto the bed. I tried to pull him away from her but my anger was not strong enough. It was tainted by heartbreak. My poor angel. I watched in agony as he attacked my angel with the broken shard of the plate. Her screams resonated deep within me. Then they were no more. She was still at last.

He would pay for what he did to my angel. I used all of the strength that I had to drag him to the top of the stairs and over to the balcony. He screamed and tried to escape but my love for her overpowered him. With the last great push of my strength I pushed him over the balcony where he fell and crashed down on a glass coffee table and wheezed pitifully until his miserable life came to an end.

'I always knew you were watching over me' I turned to see my angel standing in the doorway, her auburn hair layered perfectly on her shoulders. She approached me gently and stroked my face.

'Thank you, my love' I said as I kissed her. In that moment I was human again. I could touch her at last. She was as soft as I imagined. I held her hand as we walked down the stairs together. The door opened before us and we stepped through into the world. We were together at last. My love. Everlasting.

A BED FOR TWO

I didn't feel like getting out of bed today. I glanced outside to see a grey sky hurling the biggest drops of rain I'd ever seen. I could see the sun desperately trying to force its way through the clouds. It was straining but it was all in vain. The misery had won for now. I climbed back into bed and pulled the covers up tight. Jack was still asleep. I snuggled into his back to get warm. He held my hands as I fell into dreaming again.

After waking again, the rain had seemed to get heavier. There was no point in getting up now, I wasn't hungry, I didn't need the toilet. I was satisfied with my arms wrapped around Jack for now. The heating in the house was off but it was too cold to get out of bed to turn it on. I was freezing. I wriggled aggressively around the bed trying to get warm but staying gentle enough to not wake Jack. I gazed at his back so lovingly and daringly. He was beautiful when he slept. I stroked his back so gently. It was soft to the touch like a baby. I was content in lying here forever.

I braved getting up later in the day. I couldn't hold in my urge for the toilet any longer. I ran to the chair at the end of the bed and grabbed my dressing gown. It was not enough to warm me up. It was freezing. Every step I took on the wooden floor was agony. It was like walking on ice. I tiptoed down the corridor towards the bathroom. On my way I decided to turn on the heating in case I needed to bear this torturous journey again. It was a relief to feel the house slowly warming up around me. I decided to grab a snack and tiptoed back to bed. Jack still looked so peaceful. I tried not to disturb him as I ate my food and put a film on the television.

Another couple of hours passed and I felt tired again. I turned off the television and hurried myself under the covers. The rain had not yet subsided. It seemed to have got even stronger since I last checked. I looked out of the window from my bed to see the river outside the house. The waters had risen to a dangerous level. They were almost reaching the fence at the bottom of the garden. There was not much I could do to prevent a flood. It concerned me that our house could end up extremely damaged without anything to prevent it. I decided to think nothing more of it and headed off to sleep.

The sound of thunder rattling into my ears woke me. I looked outside to see the rain still falling hard and the river continuously rising. Jack still slept like a baby. I wrapped my arms around him again to comfort myself. He felt cold to the touch but that didn't bother me. Every time I could feel his skin against mine was heaven. It made me feel as though we were connected on another level. I felt one with him which was divine. No matter what was going on in the world around me or in my life I always felt everything disappear out of the window when Jack and I were touching. When I had my arms wrapped around him nothing could be bad. Nothing could ever be wrong.

After waking from yet another bout of sleep, it was dark outside. There was no point getting ready and out of bed at this point. I still felt tired and despite the heating being on I was still cold. I wrapped myself in the blankets further and checked to see if Jack was cold. He was very cold. I wrapped us both with the duvet and resumed my spooning of Jack.

'I love you so much. You're so beautiful when you're sleeping.' I whispered softly into his ear. He felt extremely thin as I embraced him this time. He was always quite muscular and toned but something was different. I allowed myself to sleep more since I gathered that tomorrow would be the same weather.

'Hey. I've really enjoyed this today. Sometimes it's nice to just really embrace someone for a full day. I wish we could do this every day. That would be paradise.' I muttered again into Jack's ear when I woke up. The connection we shared during this time was something otherworldly and truly magical. The rain still poured down outside. It seemed to be the middle of the night. I climbed out of bed and over to the window. I could see that the river had rose high enough that it had seeped through the fence and into our garden. The fence had become damaged in the wind and had been broken off into the river in one area. That was going to be expensive to fix. As it was the middle of the night, I decided to take action in the morning and go back to sleep.

Jack had become extremely skinny when I touched him. His soft skin was not the same. It was hard and cold. It was time to finally take action. I was saddened by the knowledge that this was goodbye, but there was nothing else I could do. I put on my dressing gown and gathered Jack up into my arms. His bones rattled and crumpled into a heap in my arms. They never seemed to last. There was nothing I could do once they were reduced to just bones. It broke my heart to let him go. I walked to the end of the back garden and lay Jack's bones gently into the flooded garden and watched him blissfully float away into the river. It really did feel like just one day this time. It really did fly by.

SLEEPING
WOOD

Sleeping Wood lies at the end of a dainty lesser-known village in the English countryside by the name of Magdalen Green. To the other side of the wood, there lies the even lesser-known village of Danton Fey. A path between the two villages slices the wood in half. The path is dark and narrow. The villagers know to never cross the Sleeping Wood. Legends and gossip circulate both villages rendering the humble folk powerless to the whispers in the trees.

Nobody knows when the Sleeping Wood became so dangerous. The first recorded tale was one hundred years ago. A young man needed to rush from Danton Fey to Magdalen Green to retrieve a doctor because his wife was giving birth. After two hours, the man's wife was unfortunately pronounced deceased due to internal bleeding and the baby was lost along with her as the doctor did not arrive. The neighbour, who was present at the birth set out to find him. They crossed through Sleeping Wood, cautiously of course. In the centre of the pathway between the villages, they found a notebook and a pen. The young man was a writer, and often wrote down his passing thoughts and adventures. The notepad read:

'I have just entered Sleeping Wood through the gate from Danton Fey. Luckily, I had the foresight to bring with me a lantern. In front of me I am shrouded in darkness. The path before me is barely visible. I am holding the torch close to my body to allow me to hold with it this notepad and write with my free hand. There is something completely ethereal about the Sleeping Wood. Everything around me does in fact seem to be sleeping. There is no life. No birdsong. No woodland creatures rustling around the leaves. I am entirely alone.'

'I venture deeper into the woods, despite my fears. Eleanor needs me more than anything. I shall not disappoint her. I see something before me. A strange yellow light. Just beyond the path. It appears to be another traveller. Perhaps they are lost. They may well need my help. I must not venture too far off course otherwise I will never get to Doctor Munro. However, my good conscience is calling for me to help. How could I not help a fellow man in need? I'm venturing off the path towards them now. The light appears closer to me as I forage through the twisting trees. I call out to my fellow traveller but nobody answers me. The light does not appear to be closing in. Perhaps they are heading the other way. I shall head back to my path and regain focus on my task. I appear to have been caught on the root of a tree. THE ROOT OF THE TREE, IT MOVES! It has me in its grasp. I cannot break free. Both of my legs are now trapped. If you find this notebook please help me. Make sure my wife is safe. Protect

90

her. Find her Doctor Munro. The roots! They do not stop! Hel-'

Ever since that fateful night people have steered clear of Sleeping Wood. Many fanatics of the Sleeping Wood point out the flaws in this narrative. Why would he keep writing if he was being attacked? How could roots attack him? Why was the notebook found in the path if he veered off? People call the believers idiotic and the subject has caused much controversy from the villagers of Magdalen Green and Danton Fey.

However, this is not the only incident involving the Sleeping Wood. Every non-believer who claims the Will-O-the-Wisp legend is a fake, who has ventured out into the darkness to prove it wrong, has never made it back to the other side. A police investigation took place in 1975 to uncover the truth behind these mysterious disappearances. Two Inspectors ventured into Sleeping Wood to look for the bodies of the missing or any clues that pointed to a culprit. They were never seen again. In response, the police closed off Sleeping Wood to the villagers and a road was built around the two villages to still make them accessible.

After the road was complete, in 1978 Sarah Dawes was driving home from work in Magdalen Green to Danton Fey. She drove alongside the Sleeping Wood. Her car suddenly stopped in the middle of the road. Some say she saw a Will-O-the-Wisp on the edge of the wood and stopped in disbelief. While her car was parked, a nearby tree suddenly fell, crushing the car with her inside it, killing her immediately. Upon investigating, police discovered that the falling tree had the police tape used to close off the Sleeping Wood had been wrapped all the way along the tree, right up to the top. The investigation concluded that the tape had been wrapped around the top of the 23 foot tree before it fell. Re-opening the investigation into the strange events.

Moving forward to 1983, three children, Bobby Drake, Jessica Lewis, and Samuel Oliver, were playing in Bobby's back garden, which ended as Sleeping Wood began. Bobby's mother, Sandra Drake, was watching the children play and observed as Bobby's ball was kicked over the fence and into the Sleeping Wood. As Sandra made her way out of the house to tell the children to leave the ball, she saw Samuel disappear through a crack in the fence that Bobby and Jessica had already climbed through. Sandra, in a rush of panic, sprinted down her long back garden and prized open the fence into Sleeping Wood. She discovered the ball on the other side of the fence and screamed the children's names. Nobody responded. She screamed and screamed but there was no sign of the children anywhere. The strangest part of Sandra's tale is that every single officer that would investigate the disappearance of the children, soon went missing not long after. To this day, Sandra still looks out of her kitchen window into Sleeping Wood and claims to see a bright yellow light coming from the spot that she found the ball her son was playing with.

The final main incident at Sleeping Wood occurred in 1993. Darren Marcus was returning home from a night out. He was extremely intoxicated and could not walk straight. He refused a taxi so his friends assumed that the fresh air would be beneficial. The legend of Darren Marcus tells that he too saw a strange yellow light emitting from Sleeping Wood and decided to pursue it. He was declared missing. In 1998, his wife, Martha, was relaxing in the home she shared with Darren when in through the front door bursts Darren himself. Darren proceeded to strangle Martha to death before suffering a heart attack and dying himself. The police discovered the bodies three days later.

In the present day, every villager knows not to travel into the Sleeping Wood. They know that the friendly and alluring lights are not what they seem. Every now and again, a brave person believes they can break the legend or discover the Will-O-the-Wisp behind the disappearances but are soon wiped from the face of the planet. A popular nursery rhyme warns the children of the dangers of Sleeping Wood.

If you travel to Sleeping Wood,

I bet you'll wish you never could.

The lights that seem to call your name,

With burning eyes as a flame,

They snatch you up nice and quick,

Any size any age, take your pick.

'I will refrain'

You must proclaim

If you want to be seen again.

RESPECT THE
DEAD

They were fifteen years old. Ryan, Peter, Isaac, and Thomas were their names. They were just naive teenage boys. They should have known better but they did not. It was just after eleven in the night. It was dark and a thick fog had descended in typical horror film fashion. The four boys had snuck out to mess around. They headed for the church at the end of the street so that they could scare each other in the graveyard. They did not mean any harm. They were just teenagers doing what teenagers do. Ryan hid behind a tombstone and jumped out at Isaac and pretended to stab him to death.

'Idiot! I could have fallen and hurt myself. I'll get you back!' Isaac giggled as he pushed Ryan off him and ran off to hide, kicking a gravestone by the name of Alexander Myles in doing so. Peter stood by the edge of the graveyard, cautious of entering out of fear and respect for the dead.

'Don't be such a wuss Peter. Get in here.' Thomas taunted Peter from the other side of a tombstone. 'Come on Peter! Are you scared the nasty ghosts are gone get you? Ooooooooooh watch out for the spoooooooky ghosts!' He mocked as he flailed his arms around like a ghost before ducking behind a tombstone and pretended to be strangled by a ghost. Peter sighed and entered the graveyard. Thomas mocked the gravestones, making childish jokes about the fact that the victims were dead and they were not and signing crude songs at them. Thomas mocked the gravestone of Mary Tyler. Ryan emerged from the fog and joined him before pulling out a football from his bag. Ryan propped his bag on the grave of Ellen Jeffords, covering up her name.

'Come on, there's a clearing over here! Let's have a kick-about.' Ryan called, Isaac and Thomas followed him eagerly and Peter dragged himself behind the others, feeling extremely uncomfortable about the whole thing. As the four kicked the ball from one to the other, Peter began to feel more confident and comfortable in the graveyard. Isaac kicked the ball to Peter, harder than he intended. Peter reacted quickly with a panic and kicked the ball away from him as quickly as he could. The ball hurtled through the air and hit an old gravestone not far from where the boys were standing. The grave was fragile and the top was cracked off by the force of the kick. A large crack began to leak its way down the side of the stone. The stone read Gareth Marley. Peter gazed at what he had done in horror. He was frozen in fear. He turned and sprinted away from the grave. The other boys followed, laughing at him. Peter picked up his bike and rode home, ignoring the other boys who taunted him.

Peter returned home and climbed back through the window he snuck out from when he left. He washed his hands in the sink and washed his face. He was as white as flour. He felt a sickly feeling deep down in his stomach. He knew what they were doing wasn't right but somehow gave in to the pressure and resorted to such horrible things because his friends had said so. That was the main problem Peter had; he never enjoyed the company of Isaac, Thomas, and Ryan anymore. They had all been friends since they were toddlers but when they all became teenagers things began to change. The other boys began to get more rebellious and aggressive, whereas Peter remained quiet and polite. He was too scared to say he didn't want to be their friend anymore. They would taunt him even more. Peter returned from the bathroom to find his bedpost had been defaced. In huge red letters, someone had written:

'rEsPeCt ThE dEaD!'

Peter rushed over and tried to wipe the writing from the bedpost but it was not possible. It didn't even smudge. He had never intended to be disrespectful to anyone. He was a good soul, he had just been misled by some bad influences. Of course Peter was capable of no harm. He was an innocent boy. He sat on his bed, tugging at his hair while staring at the message and cried until he fell asleep.

The next day was Saturday. Isaac's parents had been nagging at him for weeks to fix the curtains in his bedroom. They had fallen off when he had a girl over and was trying to sneak her out of the house without his parents seeing. He stood on a small bedside table that he had propped up against the large window. The wind blew gently on his stomach as he stretched up to reach the railing. He clipped the first of ten hooks onto the railing. He struggled to reach the top of the curtains even while standing on the table and his balance was uneasy. Two hooks. Three. Four. Five. Nearly there. Six. Seven. Eight. Nine. The bedside table snapped under Isaac's weight and he struggled to regain his footing. He toppled out of the window but managed to grab onto the window ledge to keep from falling. His grip became weak as his fingers slipped one by one from the ledge. He tried with all of his might to pull himself back up but he lost his grip completely and came tumbling down two stories to the ground, smacking his head against the tarmac pavement, killing him instantly. His curtains read:

'rEsPeCt ThE dEaD!'

A week later, Thomas was mourning the death of Isaac still. They had been the closest of the group ever since they were kids. He felt lost without his sidekick by his side. He trudged home from the fields behind his house after sitting in them and crying all day. He knew that nobody would be around so he felt safe enough to allow his feelings to break through. He had spoken briefly to Ryan and Peter at school that week but felt more comfortable when he was by himself. He held his bike very loosely as he dragged himself to the end of his road. He spotted a dog without an owner lurking at the edge of the field and decided to pet it. It always brought Thomas a sense of joy to pet an animal and he figured it may help to lift his mood from the trenches it was currently in. The dog was ragged and looked as though it was a stray. Thomas approached the raggedy dog and held out his hand to show that he meant no harm. The dog approached cautiously and sniffed the hand that was offered to him. The dog growled and before Thomas could do anything the dog lunged right at Thomas' throat, sinking its teeth right into the vein. The dog lunged and lunged as Thomas lay on the ground in a pool of his own blood. His bike read:

'rEsPeCt ThE dEaD!'

Three days later, Peter rushed up to Ryan as they were leaving school. He had a frantic look on his face that put Ryan on edge.

'Ryan! You've got to listen to me!' Peter yelled as Ryan scoffed and drooped his posture to indicate annoyance. 'That night at the graveyard. The night before Isaac died. What we did has put some sort of curse on us or something!'

'Look. I've just lost two of my best friends I'm not in the mood for this you little ferret.' Ryan shrugged as he began to walk away.

'No seriously. Isaac was the first one to disturb one of the graves. He kicked the grave of Alexander Myles. I did some research and Alexander Myles died by falling from a bridge onto a road.' Peter pleaded desperately.

'Good for Alexander. Go and bore someone else with your weird geeky homework.' Ryan walked faster as he prepared to cross the road.

'No wait! The next of us to disturb a grave was Thomas. He was mocking one of the graves and I did some research and Mary Tyler, the woman on the gravestone, was attacked and killed by her dog. Please listen to me Ryan if this is all correct then you're next. You covered the name of Ellen Jeffords who-'

'Shut it Peter before I punch you right here. Leave. Me. Alone' Ryan threatened as he began to cross the road.

'But wait she was killed by being hit by a-' Ryan was launched into the air before crashing down in a slump on the road. A car had gone speeding through a red light and hit Ryan at a speed of over 80mph. The red sports car continued driving and disappeared over the horizon. Peter rushed to Ryan's side as he lay on the ground, blood pouring from his mouth. He coughed up more blood before becoming a rigid and empty vessel as the life in him disappeared. The traffic light read:

'rEsPeCt ThE dEaD!'

Peter smashed his bedroom door open as he flustered around trying to look through his notes. Everything was true. The height. The dog. The car. In the exact order that they showed disrespect to the graves. He rummaged through pieces of paper on his desk and eventually found the death relating to Gareth Marley, the gravestone that he had smashed. He payed no attention to the masked figure sneaking up behind him with a rope in their hands. The figure grabbed Peter, wrapped the rope around his neck and tossed him out of the window, snapping his neck instantly. The masked figure looked down at the piece of paper. Next to Gareth Marley's name it read:

Cause of death: hanged by the neck until death after being found guilty of the murder of five people.'

The figure checked the tightness of the rope around Peter's bedpost. The same bedpost that read:

'rEsPeCt ThE dEaD!'

The figure left the house without being seen and entered his red sports car. In the back seat, the figure petted his scruffy-looking dog. The figure opened his glove compartment to find three screws that belonged to a bedside table and a red fountain pen. Without a word, the figure drove off into the sunset, remembering the night they had stumbled upon four teenage boys defacing a graveyard.

1 0 0

The sun was setting over the city of Pandroma. The capital city of the New World. The pristine glass buildings towered over the highest mountains and reflected the sunset, creating a beautiful illusion and a striking pattern on the glass. The World was now at peace. Pandroma was formed when the Old World crumbled due to hatred and anger. A new agenda needed to be created. An Artificial Intelligence assumed power and the world has been harmonious ever since. The Intelligence, as it was known, sought out negativity and created the perfect system to avoid it. Chester Brook, a 34 year old finance executive, leaves work in a fit of rage. A young secretary, Bethany Parker, follows him outside pleading with him for forgiveness.

'Please don't unfollow me Charlie! Please! I'm so sorry I was late again! I'm only on 100 followers! Please! I have a new-born baby! Have some compassion!' She slipped on her heel and toppled down the stairs behind him, knocking him off his feet too.

'How dare you! This suit cost me £8,000! I'm sorry but you know how the system works. I'm unfollowing you. I cannot ignore the system. I gave you ample warning to turn up on time. You chose to be late and waste my time.' He shouted back at her. He pulled a glass slab from his pocket and it ignited to life. He tapped an app labelled 'the Network' and unfollowed Bethany, bringing her follow count down to 99. Her phone began emitting a warning siren and glowing red. She began to cry as an announcement cried:

'Bethany Parker. It has come to the attention of The Intelligence that you currently possess less than 100 followers on the Network. The Network was established to keep the peace and to restore positive relationships to society. Having less than 100 followers is a crime. It shows your negative impact and un-likability among the people of Pandroma. You must now face your punishment.'

Bethany's face was now streamed with tears as she attempted to lock eyes with Chester. He could not look at her. He knew what was about to happen and he knew that making eye contact with her would humanise her, something he could not do in the circumstances. Three glass cubes flew through the air and directly towards Bethany. She tried to run but the cubes flew after her. Without a second more, the cubes fired a red laser at Bethany and she crumbled into dust on the pavement. Chester walked away as though nothing had happened. He knew the system was flawed and unfair for people who were not popular like him, but he did not care enough to do something about it as he had 22,000 followers. He was in no danger yet.

Chester made his way through the streets of Pandroma to the AirTube station. The elegant glass train arrived and

Chester boarded to head home. He lived in the most luxurious apartment building in Pandroma. The building was located in the dead centre of the city and was the tallest building, overlooking everything. The train travelled over the Freedom Lake that ran through the entire city with sapphire blue waters that sparkled like the crystal in the sunlight. Chester left the train and entered his home.

He lived in the penthouse suite right at the top of the Pride of Pandroma residential tower. He could watch every single part of the city from his pristine balcony that was perfectly decorated and maintained by his Drone servants given to him personally by The Intelligence. Chester was one of the pioneers of the Network, it was his idea to form it from the beginning. He believed that people with fewer followers were less liked and therefore the cause of negativity and the reason the world was destroyed. He received much negative press for his ideas but ultimately he succeeded and the idea was pushed through.

Chester entered the lift and travelled all the way to the 400th floor to his apartment. He slung his bag down on the luxurious leather chair that lay in his immense living room space. He commanded his drones to make him a glass of whiskey and entered out onto his balcony. The air was crisp and the perfect cooling temperature for a hot summer's day. He gazed out on the city and watched people travelling on the AirTube from work and people flocking to the many bars to celebrate the weekend. Everything was peaceful. Everything was as it should be. Chester sipped his whiskey and admired the world he had helped to create.

His phone began to vibrate in his pocket. He checked it to see that he had lost 10,000 followers on the Network. He scanned for an error but there was none to be seen. DING. Another 2,000 gone. DING. 4,000. DING 5,000. He now only had 1,000 followers. Panic filled Chester's head. What had he done wrong? He turned on his TV to see the news flashing up and his face in all of the headlines.

'Financial executive and idea smith behind the Network was seen earlier today watching gleefully at an employee's death. Surely this kind of joy at the pain of others cannot be the purpose of the Network?' The newscaster announced. Chester was furious. His face had been manipulated by the person who recorded the video. He was not gleeful at all. It deeply troubled him despite his unwillingness to intervene.

DING. 900. DING. 675. DING. 432. DING. 389. DING. 231. DING. 111. DING. 45.

'No! No! No! This can't be happening! Chester cried. It can't end like this! Not for me.' Chester threw his whiskey glass over the balcony and stormed into the house. The message blared from his phone:

'Chester Brook. It has come to the attention of The Intelligence that you currently possess less than 100 followers on the Network. The Network was established to keep the peace and to restore positive relationships to society. Having less than 100 followers is a crime. It shows your negative impact and un-likability among the people of Pandroma. You must now face your punishment.'

In a fit of rage, Chester threw his phone over the balcony too and proceeded to smash up his apartment. The glass cubes appeared and made their way towards him. He cried and begged for them not to take him but they advanced more. Suddenly, a flash of blue light struck the room and three people, faces covered by robes, appeared and shot the three cubes down. They then grabbed Chester by the arms. He kicked and screamed for them to let go and like that all four of them disappeared in the same blue flash without a trace.

After Chester was grabbed by the mysterious figures, the next thing he knew he was in some form of a dark cave. There was not much in the cave except for a desk with a series of screens and computers atop it and the three people who kidnapped him, plus a fourth robed person. The fourth kidnapper removed his robes to reveal a bearded man, aged around 35. He was in quite muscular physique and tall in stature.

'Hello Chester.' He spoke in a deep, gruff tone. 'My name is Angeles. You might remember me for being the first person to ever escape the death penalty for having less than 100 followers on the Network.' The other three kidnappers removed their robes.

'This is Calista, Marco, and Lapis. They also all escaped the death penalty. We developed a technology together that cloaks us from the Network and The Intelligence. I was the first to test it out and it worked. We've been hiding out in Mount December for a year now. We are undetectable to the system.'

'Why have you brought me here? I'll have you found! I created the Network!' Chester shouted and tried to break free of Calista and Lapis' grasp.

'We need you Chester. Long before we were excommunicated we have been devising a plan to overthrow The Intelligence and putting a stop to the Network for good.'

Calista chimed in. She released Chester from her grasp and made her way over to the computers. 'I bet you were wondering who recorded you and sent it in to the media? The reason you lost all of your followers. It was us.'

'Why? How dare you mess with my system! It works. There hasn't been disagreement since it was introduced! I'm a revolutionary!' Chester arrogantly announced.

'Except you haven't fixed anything.' Lapis added as she released him from her grasp. 'You can't escape. You're wanted for the death penalty as we speak.' She joined Calista at the computers.

'There have been 4,432 unjustified deaths due to the Network this year. When you created the Network did you even think of people who suffer from anxiety? Who cannot go out and make friends because of their illness. There were 324 people who suffered from anxiety killed this month. What about people who manipulate the truth? Like we did to you. Innocent people are killed because of the manipulation of others. 1,234 deaths of that nature occurred this month. Did you think of any of this?' Lapis shrugged her shoulders and turned her back to Chester. She was right. He had never considered that side of things when he introduced the idea. Guilt suddenly overcame him.

'You're completely right. How can I help?' Chester rose and walked over to the screens.

'We believe to stop the Network we need access to The Intelligence, which we figured you would probably have the best chance at doing so. We thought the only way you would agree to help us was if you faced death yourself.' Angeles rejoined the conversation. 'We need you to infiltrate The

Intelligence inside the Harmony Building and reprogram it and delete the Network from its systems for good. We will be able to help you get into the city undetected and protect you if we are discovered.' This was all a lot for Chester to comprehend. But he reluctantly agreed and the group set off immediately.

In Pandroma, Chester arrived at the main city AirTube station with Angeles, Calista, Lapis, and Marco. They moved quickly among the crowds to avoid detection from Watcher Drones, the new and updated form of CCTV. Each wore a bracelet constructed by Angeles to hide them from the Network so that the cubes could not detect them. Chester was still feeling guilty at the fact that his idea had caused so much pain and went so very wrong. He had wasted all of his work.

They approached the Harmony Building and Angeles tricked the Identification to allow them access. As they made their way through the lobby, a red light flashed across the room and a warning message blared out:

'WARNING. UNAUTHORISED PERSONAL DETECTED. IDENTIFICATION: ANGELES VARADI. CALISTA AUGUST. CHESTER BROOK. LAPIS ANDERSON. MARCO LAZUL TERMINATION IMMINENT.'

'They found us! Let's move!' Angeles cried as the five proceeded to run through the lobby and over to the lift. Six cubes entered the lobby and began shooting at the trespassers. Marco returned fire and disabled one of them. Chester, Angeles, Calista, and Lapis boarded the lift and called out to Marco to hurry. As he was about to enter the lift, Marco was reduced to a pile of dust by the cubes. Angeles forced the doors to the lift closed as they escaped. Calista over-rid the security lock on the lift, allowing them to travel.

The lift reached the top floor of the Harmony Building and entered swiftly. Just as they did, the cubes appeared down one of the corridors and began pursuing the group. The cubes struck Lapis, turning her to dust as well. They reached the corridor to enter the chamber of The Intelligence just as the cubes began to draw in. Angeles quickly hacked into the security of the door while Calista shot at the cubes. She took down two but more seemed to appear behind them. Angeles broke through the door and pulled Chester through with him.

'I'll hold off the cubes! You two are more important to this mission. This needs to be done. Good luck!' Said Calista as she pulled the door closed behind her. After much shooting and fighting a ferocious scream was heard before the shooting was silenced. Angeles paused to mourn the loss of Calista before heading to the heart of The Intelligence. A massive array of wires and hard-drive filled the room.

'It's this way to the programming of the Network.' Chester ushered Angeles towards a large display of wires and code near the centre of The Intelligence. Chester got to work on re-coding while Angeles stayed look out and shot down any incoming cubes. Chester fumbled and typed and typed until eventually he was done.

'There, it's done.' Chester said with lumbering heavy breaths. Angeles approached him and patted him on the back in a congratulatory manner. Chester smiled at Angeles before elbowing Angeles in the stomach and stealing his gun. He pointed the gun at Angeles and prepared to fire.

'What the hell are you doing Chester?' Angeles cried. The betrayal in his voice was not subtle.

'I reprogrammed the Network so that my follower count had been restored to its former number, 22,000. I also added a line of coding that makes it impossible to unfollow me. Making me invincible. You really thought I'd sacrifice years of work because of your little guilt trip? Hah! Long live the Network!' Chester declared as he shot Angeles in the chest, killing him immediately. Chester left the Harmony Building with a smile on his face and returned back to his apartment and poured himself another glass of whiskey.

PIGGY

Here we go again. Another one of his rants. I'd just sat down. I returned from feeding the pigs and started the kettle boiling. I was dying for a lovely cuppa. It was a hot day, the perfect weather for shovelling pig crap and listening to another one of Lee's rants. I'm seventy-six now, I don't have much life left to waste.

'Have you seen this on the telly love? Two bloody men prancing around like they own the world. I don't know how these bloody perverts are allowed to just roam the streets. Bring back the days when they were stoned in prison or something of the sort. I do not want to see that disgusting display in my living room. I fought in the war you know!' There it was. Always the war. He went to the war in 1945 a week before the thing was finished. He wasn't exactly the saviour of the free world. You'd think the amount he goes on about the war he personally defeated Hitler. Arse. The kettle started to get lukewarm

'To top it all off guess what? One of them's oh what are you supposed to say now? Ethnic. I miss the days you could call them exactly what they were. Either way they should all bugger off back to where they came from. Disgusting creatures. They aren't people.' Ah yes Lee is also a racist. As if he didn't already have so much going for him as it was. Pig. No not a pig, my pigs were beautiful creatures with more intelligence to not be bothered by something as minimal as race or sexuality. He was a rat. With less sexual appeal. When we got married things weren't much different. I married him because I'd just turned thirty, and to be an unmarried woman at thirty people started to ask questions. Not that I cared. I just wanted my parents off my back so I married the first man I saw. Unfortunately that man was Lee. Look at him sat on that sofa, I thought, a lazy, degenerate who's worth no good to anybody. I paid his ridiculous comments no mind and wiped down the table as the kettle began to heat up. I needed this cuppa. Or something stronger.

'Where's my cuppa woman? Bloody hell you're slow. You're meant to provide for me you know? Your sole purpose is to see to my needs and you can't even bloody do that. Honestly that's another thing we need to get rid of. Lazy women who can't even see to me right. Look at you sat there on your arse doing nothing. Go do some washing or something.' The trifecta, sexist, racist, and homophobic. I often didn't speak out against his horrid behaviour towards me. I just imagined a life where I was allowed to have friends and we would go dancing and get a little too drunk for our age and have a brilliant time. Sipping margaritas by a pool in some hot country with my best girlfriends and a good book. No men for miles around. Rising to Lee's ridiculous comments would just entice an argument further which, at my age, isn't something I felt like I needed. The kettle was now nearly ready.

'Are you listening to me woman? Do something instead of sitting there ignoring me! Rude cow. I married you. That means you treat me like a god. Get me some food!' Today I felt different. Something new inside me came to life. A streak of rebelliousness. No, I wasn't going to get him something to eat. He could get off his fat arse and get it himself. He had legs. I think. Under that heaping mound of a stomach. I continued to sit at the table and wait for the kettle to boil, which had just started to bubble.

'Don't you dare ignore me you tamp! Oi! Listen to me when I am talking to you!' He shouted louder and spat in my direction in doing so. How very graceful. Maybe today was the day to speak up. Why not. I'd wasted forty-six years of my life sitting quietly. He rose from his seat. Hallelujah. He plodded over to me and slammed his hands down on the table.

'Is something the matter dear?' I said as sweet as a button. I gave him a loving smile.

'Where is my food! How dare you ignore me! Get me my food! Do you want me to starve?'

'Oh I don't think that's possible dear, you've got plenty of fat in reserve.'

That was it. I'd done it. Finally. I argued back for the first time in forty-six years. It felt so liberating. I could see a large blue vain throbbing in his temple. He was enraged. I was delighted. The Kettle had now boiled.

'What did you just say to me? How dare you give me lip when I've provided everything for you. You ugly old bitch.' He slapped me right across the face. That didn't bother me. It wasn't the first time. 'Now where is my bloody cup of tea?' He screamed

'It's here darling!' I said extremely gently as I lifted the boiling kettle and smashed it right into the throbbing blue vein in his temple. He screamed and fell to the floor and it felt so good that I did it again. Again. Again. Again.

I finally made that cup of tea. It felt very refreshing. I'd just been out and fed the pigs again. I don't normally give them meat but they certainly enjoyed it. They just couldn't stop gobbling it up. Good thing too as there's plenty of it left in the freezer. It was nice to have a bit of peace and quiet around here.

JUST SURVIVE THE NIGHT

It's just passed midnight. You regret coming home this late more than anything. All you want is to be back in your bed, snuggled up ready for sleep. The road is pitch black, you can see nothing in front of you. Your headlights are on but they provide no relief to the seemingly endless darkness surrounding you. You can see the lights flashing on the trees as you pass through the woodland road. The woodland seems to go on forever. Paranoid, you keep checking your back seat because the way light keeps shining on the back seat makes it look like someone was sitting there.

The engine of your car begins to stutter. You knew you should have stopped that petrol station a little while down the road. You knew the petrol was running low. It was just a sense of cockiness. You believed it would last. The car is getting slower and slower as you venture further into the wilderness. Your heart drops into your stomach. There is nothing around you. Entire wilderness. You have never felt so isolated and alone. Where the hell are you? The car has now fully come to a stop. In the middle of nowhere.

No phone signal. Naturally. You need help. You decide to wait in your car for a passing commuter. Three hours later, not a single car has passed. You decide to exit your car to try and find the nearest house or petrol station or anything that showed a single sign of life. You're going to have to venture into the woods to find someone. There is nothing on either side of the road as far as you can see. At last. A light. Off in the distance. It appears to be coming from a small cabin. How cliché you think to yourself. A cabin in the woods and a broken down car. If you are going to be in a horror film you'd at least like to be payed.

The cabin is small and extremely run down but you hope at least they will have a phone. You approach the rustic wooden door and give it a light knock. The door opens to reveal an extremely burly male with a ragged figure. He is unkempt but could easily overpower you if needed.

'Hello. I'm so sorry. My car has run out of petrol and I was wondering if I could use your phone?' You say to the man. No reply. Wonderful. He just stares at you with a dormant expression. There is nothing behind his icy stare. After multiple attempts you decide your attempts are futile and bid the man goodbye and decide to return to your car.

You make your way back through the forest of your nightmares. The leaves rustle beneath your shoes. Aside from that silence falls among everything. Your small torch lights the path before you but everything else remains bathed in darkness. All of a sudden that is not the only noise you can here. There is another set of footprint noises. Following you.

Not too far behind. You swivel to see nothing behind you. The dim light from the cabin gives a slight illumination of the surroundings. A shadow staggers behind a tree trunk. That's it you think. Time to pick up the pace. You begin a quick pace through the winding trees only to hear you are not the only one. The man from the cabin is lurking behind you in the trees. You see his muscular physique. You see the axe.

You have to escape. Your first thought is to just run. Naturally, it begins to rain heavily, making the floor around you slippery and dangerous. The determination to escape deep down within allows you to somehow transform into a ninja as you glide over the slippery mud. He's running too. A lot faster than you. You can't help but checking behind you to see if he is catching up, which he always is. You hear his raspy breath getting closer to you. Closer still. You can feel it on the back of your neck. That's when you fall. Flat into the mud. You are stuck. The man looms over you and raises his axe. Terror sweeps your entire body as you realise this is it, this is your demise. In a last glimmer of hope, you manage to free yourself from the mud and roll to your side just as the axe comes crashing down on what would have been your head.

The man jolts his head to see you as you rise to your feet, struggling like Bambi when he was first born. The axe swings again, narrowly missing your chest. Run! You think. Get out of here, but where was there to go? Your car wasn't working and there was no way for miles that you could go. You were doomed. THE PETROL STATION. It must have been miles down the road but at least it was a destination. There would be people there who weren't going to swing an axe at you. You begin to run in the direction that you remember the petrol station being in. You run faster than you've ever run before.

You look behind you to see how far away your murderer is to find he is nowhere to be seen. You've outrun him. At last. You stop to catch your breath and examine the area with your torch to find that the man is no longer on your tail. He has disappeared completely. A rustle in the trees alerts you to shine your torch behind you. The light illuminates the trees to find nothing there. The light trembles with your hand. The rain still pours around you, leaving you drenched and freezing cold. You swivel around with yourself and your torch. HIM. He's there. Right in front of your face. He's practically touching you. A small scream leaves your petrified mouth as you stand frozen in fear, staring right into the nightmarish face of the axeman. He raises his axe to stake but you push him at the last second and make an exit in the direction of the petrol station. He follows so close behind you. So close. You have never had such a rush of adrenaline in your life. All you want to do is lie down and cry. Never in your life have you been so horrified. The sound of you running is matched with a faster rhythm of the axeman sprinting after you. You manage to keep a good distance between the two of you but he always manages to close in.

Winding. Twisting. You run through the hellish labyrinth of the forest. Your legs are in so much pain but you can't stop. Not now. Not with a deranged lunatic hunting your every move. THE LIGHT. You can see it. The petrol station is right there. You've made it. You've survived. You burst through the doors of the petrol station.

'HELP ME! My car has broken down and a man is trying to murder me with an axe!' You scream at a surprised cashier.

'Slow down there, what do you mean?' He responds in a surprisingly calm tone for someone who just heard what he did. 'You must mean Billy. Yeah, he's always had a screw or two loose. Then again don't we all?' The cashier says as he fumbles around for something underneath the till. The bell dings behind you as you hear the door slam closed. You are currently too fixated on the cashier and tired to turn around. The cashier returns to his standing position and grins.

'Here they are Billy. I knew how much you wanted this one.' He chuckles as he pulls out an axe from underneath the till. You turn to find Billy the axeman glaring down at your face. This was a set up. You are left helpless when both men approach you and corner you, axes at the ready. They raise their axes towards you, both laughing hysterically and everything goes black.

THE INVASION

We have nearly arrived. I've heard so much about The Planet. We can see it sometimes from the surface of our planet. They used to tell us stories of strange beings that lived there called Aliens. Nobody from my planet had ever travelled to there before. I was lucky enough to be on the first exploratory craft. There were five of us on the Planet expedition. Myself, my nickname is Zo, Commander Xi, Medical Officer Xa, Research Officer Se, and Combat Expert, Ka. I was the pilot. We all went by nicknames. We were each given a two letter nickname at the start of the expedition to protect our identities in case anything went wrong. I had been training for this day ever since I graduated. I had always been so fascinated by the Planet and it was my dream to meet the Aliens and build relations with them.

'Thirty minutes until landing.' I announced to the rest of the crew. We approached the Planet's atmosphere and passed through. I had been advised to not land in the water as the stories say that Aliens live on land. We were landing on a small island that they hailed as one of their biggest superpowers. Commander Xi had been observing the Aliens for over 50 years. He was the one that passed on the information that became stories. I could not believe that we were finally going to make contact with the Aliens.

'Right here's the plan' Commander Xi announced as we gathered around. 'I will lead the way with Research Officer Se following beside me. Pilot Zo and Combat Expert Ka you will follow behind and be on the lookout for threatening behaviour. Medical Officer Xa, you will remain behind us. We need you to be protected in case of any danger. Does everyone understand me?' We all nodded in agreement and prepared for landing.

I made a landing in a small field outside the main city that they called their capital. Commander Xi prepared us all and we began backing resources that we might need to survive. He attached to each of us a patch containing some of our home planet's atmosphere so that we could survive in the Planet's atmosphere.

I looked out of the visor in the front of our ship to see hundreds of Aliens gathering outside our ship. They had metal contraptions that were pointed at us and a metal machine with some sort of caterpillar tracks and a large snout, like our tanks but not quite. I wondered what that was. The Aliens looked different than I had imagined. They were small and pink. The Aliens shouted something at our ship. I did not understand what they said. We did not have the capacity to translate them.

The door to the ship opened and I was filled with excitement as we stepped out. I could not believe I was going to make contact with Aliens. Commander Xi stepped out and addressed the crowds of Aliens waiting outside for us. He gave them a courteous wave and began to speak to them.

'Hello! We come here in peace. We do not want any harm. We only seek to build a friendship between our two planets. I am Commander Xi! These are my crew. May we speak to your leaders?' He saluted the crowd as we waited for a response. A member of the crowd stepped forward and uttered something incomprehensible to us. He then pulled out a metal device and pointed it at Commander Xi. He pressed something on the device that fired out at Commander Xi. He shrieked out and fell to the floor in pain and died. I was horrified. I had always believed that the Aliens would embrace us but they were attacking us. What were we to do?

Combat Expert Ka fired his weapon at the Alien that Killed Xi as me and Se gathered around Xa to protect her. We tried to get her back onto the ship but the Aliens fired things at it and the emergency protection initiative activated, closing the doors. We decided to try and find cover somewhere but there was nowhere for us to run. The Aliens killed Ka and began shooting at the three of us. They killed Se and ran after Xa and I. We tried to escape. We ran for our lives. They were faster than we were and grabbed a hold of us. They began to electrocute the two of us and tie us down. I struggled to escape but I couldn't. We were both trapped.

They tied us both up and put us in the back of a strange vehicle. We travelled for several days and transferred between multiple strange vehicles. I had never been so scared. We had been reassured that the Aliens were peaceful like us but they were nothing like us. They were savages with an inferior and barbaric society. Luckily, I was still being transported with Xa. She had a terrified look in her eyes the same as I did. I tried to reassure her. It didn't work. I think because I didn't believe it myself.

We finally arrived at a stationary location. The Aliens dragged Xa and I out of the transportation and into a strange metal building. It looked like some sort of bunker. They took us into a large white room filled with bright lights and what appeared to be medical equipment. What happened next truly horrified me.

They began to cut Xa while she was still alive. They observed her screaming and yet still continued to torment her. They drilled into her while she was still alive and cut her open. They began to remove her organs and experiment on them. They removed her organs one by one. She had been dead for days. They didn't care. They took limb from limb. Tearing at her flesh until she was nothing more than a couple traces of blood on a laboratory table. I wanted to be sick. The Aliens were truly disgusting beings.

As for me, they observed my emotional responses and tested my behaviour in various situations. They deprived me of food. They hurt me. They tortured me. They kept me as a show. I was locked in a cell for the rest of my life. Every day they came back with a new torture method. They never stopped. The torture perpetuated eternally. Every day I became weaker. Every day I longed for my home a lot more. I learned the Aliens called themselves Humans and the Planet was in fact called Earth. Every day I grew to hate the Humans more and more. I longed to be back on Mars. I was safe there.

C O N S C I O U S N E S S

Work was a drag. I worked in a Fried Chicken Shop called 'Chicken Boy' because they were a cheap knockoff of KFC. I hated my job. I wanted to quit every day, but it paid the rent, just about, so I decided to stick it out. I didn't really have a plan for the future. I dropped out of University so jobs like this were all I could get really. I was satisfied with my mediocre life. Except I wasn't. I hated it. I just couldn't be bothered changing anything. That was my main problem really. I was too lazy to be involved in anything. I just sat back and let things happen for me.

I finished my shift at 12 and closed up the shop as normal. It took me around an hour to turn off the fat fryers and swept around. Jai had decided to leave early so he could go get stoned and hook up with some girl. He did that every shift. I specifically asked to not be put on shifts with him anymore but Deisha didn't care. I think she liked to torture me a little. I closed up the front of the shop and made my way home. I got the bus to Brixton and began to walk to my flat. It was always scary being out at this time in Brixton. I kept my head down and listened to music.

I was passing a small field of green when I saw a young girl walking towards me. A man in a black mask and a black hoodie creeped up behind her and grabbed her around the mouth. He pulled out a knife from his hoodie and stabbed her repeatedly in the chest. I froze in shock. I should call the police. I really should. I wanted to. I couldn't. What if he got me too? The girl called out for my help but I ignored her. Like I said, I was too lazy to be involved in anything. I couldn't. I turned back and headed home another way instead.

The scenario played in my mind all the way home. I hurried and persisted to check behind me to see if I was being followed. I did not want to end up like the girl. I entered my flat and repeatedly checked the door was locked behind me. I went to bed and thought about the expression on the girl's face as she screamed in pain. I should have done something. I really wished I had. Different scenarios played in my mind. If I had been brave and saved her. If I had called the police. If I had been killed too. I had just watched someone get murdered and did nothing about it.

I was woken at around 3 in the morning by someone shuffling around in my room. I turned the light on and was horrified to see the girl that had been murdered standing beside my bed. She was pale and her eyes looked as though she hadn't slept in days. The stab marks remained on her chest and spots of blood covered her shirt. It must be a dream. She must have died. She was dead. She was dead. I shook my head and pinched myself but she didn't go away.

'What do you want! I'm sorry okay! I'm sorry. Leave me alone.' I shouted at her. She didn't move. Her black eyes locked on me. 'Come on. What is it? You're gonna haunt me for the rest of my life. Is that it? Well fine. Do what you want.' Again, nothing from her. I ignored her presence as she watched me and tried to sleep. Every ten minutes or so, I checked back up on her to see if she was still there and every single time she was. Glaring at me with those eyes. It was driving me insane.

A week passed. Every single moment of my life, she was there. I got up, she was there. I showered with her watching me. I went to work and she followed me. I went home she sat next to me on the bus home. She watched me as I was sleeping. Every second of my life she forced herself into. I tried everything to get her out of my mind. Nothing moved her. I mean nothing. I grew tired. I couldn't sleep at night because of her watching me. I figured that she was a manifestation of my guilt. I didn't know how to get rid of a manifestation. I was going insane.

The weeks flew by. Of course, she was still there. Her name was Alisha Johnson. I attended her funeral and placed some flowers down at the site of her death. Her killer was her ex-boyfriend, she broke up with him and he felt entitled to her so he murdered her. He was sentenced to thirteen years in prison. I visited her grave and placed flowers there for her. None of this stopped her from haunting my every move. I never heard her speak. She never changed her expression. Many times, I lashed out at her and told her to leave me alone. She never did. My life had spiralled downwards ever since. I was on my final warning at work. I couldn't focus and I had shouted at customers because I have slept for around 1 hour a night. I can't go on for much longer.

I was working an afternoon shift. I dragged myself to the bus stop to get the bus. Alisha followed me every step of the way. Wearing down my soul with every step she took. I tried to fall asleep on the bus but there she was. Endless blank staring preventing me from living my life. I arrived at work, late. It took me longer to do everything because I was so tired. Deisha had put herself on the shift with me today so that she could monitor me. As if I needed another monitor.

'Why are you being so slow? These customers need their chicken. Hurry up. Why are you so lazy? This is not the place to relax. You have a job to do.' She yelled and yelled and yelled at me. All day. Every single thing I tried to do she shouted at me for doing it wrong. I couldn't win.

'You are doing that wrong. Stop that.' Constantly in my ear. Alisha constantly in my eye-line. I was so tired. I was losing basic bodily functions. I stared at the fryer as the chicken was cooking. All I did was stare because I was too tired to do anything else. I could feel myself slipping into sleep. My arms flopped by my side. Deisha's shouting became a distant mumble as I drifted off. I relaxed myself and allowed myself into sleep. The next thing I knew I was in immense pain. My head was on fire. The sound of sizzling ran through my ears. I was surrounded by boiling hot liquid. It burned so much. I was being fried. Then there was an overwhelming darkness as I entered into nothingness. It was bliss.

A LONG WALK HOME

He was standing at York Piccadilly at 8:05 P.M. while his girlfriend boarded the X47 bus from York to Hull. She was travelling to Bishop Burton. A quaint typical English village near the East Coast with picturesque views and an appealing pub named the Altisidora.

They were a lovely couple. He kissed her on the cheek to say goodbye. He was so tender towards her. He thought the world of her. She thought the world of him. It was the perfect couple. Of course, they were both only young, in University in fact. He waited for her to take her seat before waving very lovingly and heading back home. It was a cold winter night. It was a dangerous night in fact.

There had been murders in York around the time. Particularly students. The bodies were always found in the river. Often blamed as drunken students falling on their way home from the popular nightclubs that were mostly on the opposing side of the river. It was a risky thing for a student to be walking on his own on a night like this.

He placed his hands in his pockets after rubbing them together to get himself warm. He turned the corner and passed Marks and Spencer's before stopping outside the Golden Fleece Inn. He read the sign in the doorway claiming to be England's most haunted pub and snickered slightly at the pub's appearance on 'Most Haunted'. He proceeded to walk inside and bought at a drink at the bar from his friend who worked there. It was Monday, which meant that there was £1 off draught beer. He mingled with his friend at the bar and laughed together.

After he finished his pint, he said his goodbyes to his friend and left the pub. Heading up the Shambles, he sent a text to his girlfriend laughing about the fact that there were three Harry Potter shops all next door to each other. He continued up the Shambles, which at this time was entirely empty and had quite a ghostly other-worldly feel to it. He felt as though he had stepped into an alternate realm. It brought a shiver up his spine.

He was a tall young man. Around six foot. He had the slightest beard that appeared to be more stubble-ish than a real beard but it suited his darker complexion. He was a popular student. Everyone seemed to want to be around him. He wasn't much the joker type but more the sweet type that everyone seemed to rely on as a friend. He was a nice person.

After exiting the ghost dimension that was the Shambles, he entered into King's Square. A street performer from earlier in the day had left a few props and the performance space markings laid around to further add to the desolation of the city at the time. He was wary and careful. He checked around at all times to make sure he wasn't being watched or followed. Little did he know he was being watched all the time. By someone who was far too much of a sleuth to be noticed by him, despite his intelligence.

Instead of keeping to the streets that contained the odd person visiting a bar, he walked through St. Andrewgate, a small residential street that lead to the Bartle Garth snickelway. A dangerous move for someone being prowled by a ruthless killer. For a student who was surrounded by an abundance of isolation. Every curtain in the houses was drawn. Every blind shut. He was entirely alone in this mythical world of the night time. He had been so careful until he made this conscious decision to avoid the drunken people of York.

As he made his way through the desolation, he began to become conscious that he was not the only one walking this route. His pace quickened. His breathing became slightly erratic. He was terrified. Of course, there was good reason to be terrified. There was also no reason to be suspicious. However, there were only two people walking an obscure path together, there was also every right to be suspicious. He was running now. Doing anything he could to make sure he was in the presence of other people to comfort himself.

He made it. He was through the snickelway and into the street where there were enough people to comfort his racing heart. Two men stood outside Ambiente Tapas smoking a cigarette. At Monkbar, two drunk women staggered about the street, obviously coming from Keystones. He was at peace. There was nothing that could harm him in front of others.

He proceeded to York St John University, he lived there on the Lord Mayor's Walk campus. Block A.

The Student Union was bustling at this time. Students were gathered in their masses for the student night, Kuda Monday, one of the more popular events. He passed down the side of the union, where a group of windows allowed him to gaze at the students getting drunk and having fun. His block entrance was directly in front of him down the path that he was walking. He passed the chapel, bathed in complete darkness. There was a light on in his block. That brought a comfort to him because it meant that he was not arriving back to everyone being out. He approached the door and got out his keys. They were stuck in his pocket and he fumbled around to find the right key.

That's when I did it. The opportune moment arose in front of me. I dashed down the path and put my hands around his neck. I had been observing him for a while and eventually decided that he would be the perfect next victim. It was me that he spotted following him but that didn't stop me. I tugged harder around his neck as he struggled. He gasped for breath and attempted to scream for help but nothing could escape his mouth. It was a shame. He was such a nice boy. His girlfriend would be heartbroken. A true tragedy. I just couldn't let my decisions go. Once I chose someone they had to go. The breath slowly escaped his body and he became limp in my arms.

Thank you for reading my stories. Stay tuned to the website to hear more coming very soon. Happy nightmares!

abramacabre.wordpress.com

Printed in Great Britain
by Amazon